BOOK 1: THE CURSE OF THE BOLOGNA SANDWICH
In which superhero Melvin Beederman and third-grader Candace Brinkwater team up to stop bad guys in Los Angeles.

BOOK 2: THE REVENGE OF THE McNASTY BROTHERS
In which the McNasty Brothers escape from prison to get revenge on Melvin and his partner in uncrime, Candace.

BOOK 3: THE GRATEFUL FRED
In which Melvin and Candace must find who is out to get rock star Fred of The Grateful Fred.

Coming Soon:

BOOK 4: DOOM WITH A VIEW

MELVIN BEEDERMAN SUPERHERO

THE CURSE OF THE BOLOGNA SANDWICH

GREG TRINE

ILLUSTRATED BY
RHODE MONTIJO

HENRY HOLT AND COMPANY ★ NEW YORK

For Juanita
—G. T.

For my brother Michael
—R. M.

Henry Holt and Company, LLC
Publishers since 1866
175 Fifth Avenue, New York, New York 10010
www.henryholtchildrensbooks.com

Henry Holt® is a registered trademark of Henry Holt and Company, LLC.
Text copyright © 2006 by Greg Trine
Illustrations copyright © 2006 by Rhode Montijo
All rights reserved. Distributed in Canada by H. B. Fenn and Company Ltd.

Library of Congress Cataloging-in-Publication Data
Trine, Greg.
The curse of the bologna sandwich
Greg Trine ; illustrated by Rhode Montijo.–1st hardcover and pbk. eds.
p.   cm.–(Melvin Beederman, superhero)
Summary: After graduating from the Superhero Academy, Melvin Beederman
heads for Los Angeles, where he unexpectedly teams up with Candace
Brinkwater, school play actress, to nab the evil McNasty Brothers.
ISBN-13: 978-0-8050-7928-9 / ISBN-10: 0-8050-7928-9 (hardcover)
1   3   5   7   9   10   8   6   4   2

ISBN-13: 978-0-8050-7836-7 / ISBN-10: 0-8050-7836-3 (paperback)
1   3   5   7   9   10   8   6   4   2

[1. Heroes–Fiction. 2. Los Angeles (Calif.)–Fiction. 3. Humorous stories.]
I. Montijo, Rhode, ill. II. Title. III. Series.
PZ7.T7356Cu 2006   [Fic]–dc22   2005013997
First Edition–2006 / Book designed by Donna Mark and Laurent Linn
Printed in the United States of America on acid-free paper. ∞

CONTENTS

NEVER SAY NO
TO A CRY FOR HELP

Melvin Beederman didn't feel like a
superhero. Sure, he'd graduated from
the Superhero Academy with the others.
And he did look fantastic in his red
cape and high boots.
But there were some
things that bothered
him. He never once was
able to leap a tall building
in a *single* bound; it always

1

took him five or six tries. Stopping a speeding locomotive wasn't easy. And that whole x-ray vision thing—it brought nothing with it but guilt. Everywhere Melvin looked—underwear.

Still, he was fast. He was good at math and science. And he had so impressed his teachers with his oral report on the nature of good and evil that he nudged Superhero Carl out of the top spot—Carl who was a single-leap building jumper and who had no problem stopping trains.

Melvin Beederman beat him out. He graduated at the top of his class.

Perhaps Headmaster Spinner had said it best: "Your brain is your greatest weapon." And he had high hopes for young Beederman.

Now that graduation was over, Melvin made his way across the school yard, past the exercise area where Super-hero Carl was busy bench-pressing a

Buick. Carl stopped what he was doing long enough to sneer and said, "The top of our class. Bah! You can't even stop a train."

"I can so. It just takes me a while," Melvin said.

He knew Carl was still angry about being bumped out of the top spot. Carl was being sent far away for his first assignment, all the way to the Fiji Islands, and Melvin was glad. He didn't trust Carl any farther than he could throw a Chevrolet . . . or a Buick, for that matter.

"Where are they sending you?" Carl asked.

"Don't know yet. I'm meeting with the headmaster in a few minutes."

Headmaster Spinner was waiting for Melvin at the door to his office. His belly was huge, and Melvin wondered how he ever got off the ground. Did *he* have a hard time leaping tall buildings?

"Come in, Melvin," he said. "Well, today is the day. Are you ready to start your life of fighting crime?"

Melvin wasn't sure. It had been two years since he'd been plucked from the orphanage—two years of flying lessons, of stopping trains, of seeing through walls. And now he was being sent off to save the world. How could he tell the headmaster he didn't think he was up to it?

"Where are you sending me, sir?" he asked finally.

"Before we get to that, tell me, do you have any questions? Any problems you'd like to discuss?"

"Well . . . ," Melvin began.

"Yes?"

"The x-ray vision. I had no idea there were so many kinds of underwear in the world."

"You'll learn to turn it off with time." The headmaster spun around. "But as long as we're on the subject, what do you think of my striped boxers?"

"I was trying to ignore them, sir."

"Right. Let's get down to business. I'm sending you to Los Angeles, California. They haven't had a superhero there since Kareem Abdul-Jabbar retired."

"Who's that?"

"Famous basketball player."

"What about Shaquille O'Neal?" Melvin asked.

"He's not a superhero. He's just very tall." He noticed the worried look on the boy's face. "They need you over there, Melvin. Remember, what's the first rule of the Superhero's Code?"

" 'Never say no to a cry for help.' "

"Correct. You'll leave immediately. Do well and you can have your choice of assignments."

Did he have to bring up the code? The code had been so drummed into the students of the academy that everyone knew it by heart. Someone was crying out for help, and Melvin knew he couldn't say no.

"The code will guide you," Headmaster Spinner said. He led Melvin out of his office onto the lawn and shook his hand. "Now get going."

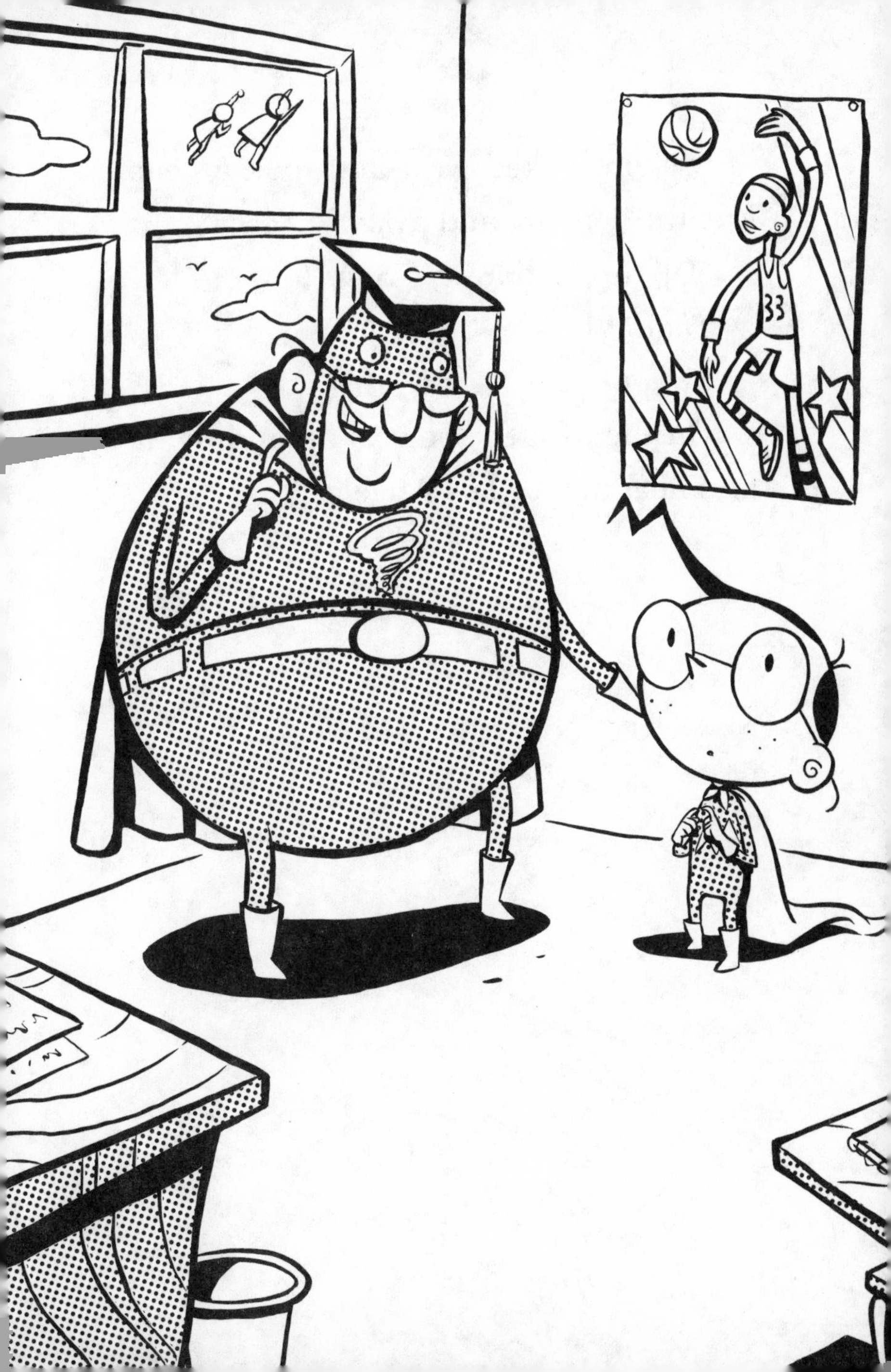
33

Melvin looked west and took a deep breath. "Up, up, and away." *Crash!*

"Up, up, and away." *Splat!*

Thud!

Kabonk!

On the fifth try, he was up and flying and heading for Los Angeles.

FIND A GOOD HIDEOUT

Once he was up and flying, Melvin Beederman wasn't coming down for anybody. Not until he got to Los Angeles—3,000 miles away.

Let's see, if a superhero flies 500 miles an hour, how long will it take to go 3,000 miles? Doing math in the air was Melvin's favorite hobby. It was almost as much fun as dropping water balloons on Superhero Carl.

Almost.

But flying for six hours was about five and a half hours longer than he had ever flown at one time. He might be too tired to catch bad guys when he got to Los Angeles. How embarrassing for the academy. How embarrassing for Melvin Beederman!

Melvin spotted a jet nearby. He flew over to it and knocked on the pilot's window.

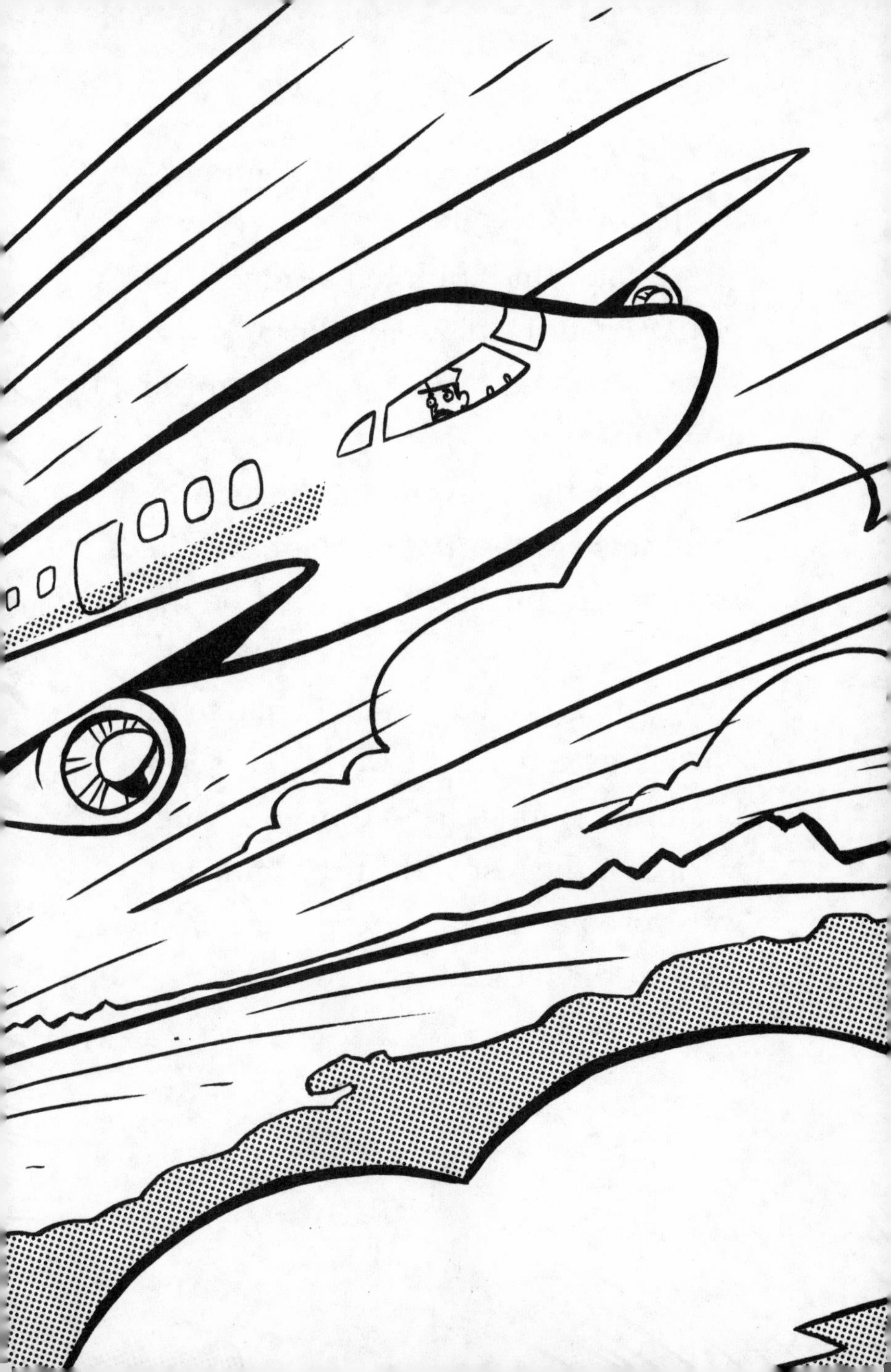

"Where are you heading, Captain?"

"Los Angeles."

"Great. Mind if I hitch a ride?"

"Are you the new superhero?"

"Yes," Melvin said. "This is my first assignment."

"I hear they haven't had a superhero there since Kareem Abdul-Jabbar retired. Have a seat on the wing. We'll be there in a jiffy."

"Thanks, Captain." Melvin had to save his energy. Saving the world was serious business. And so he sat on the wing of the jet for the rest of the trip, doing fancy word problems in his head and making faces at the passengers.

Melvin thought only bad guys had hide-outs. And he was no bad guy. Still, it was part of the code: "Find a good hideout." And so, as soon as he got to Los Angeles, he set about to do just that.

Melvin looked around.

Holy skyscrapers! he thought. *This place is huge.*

Holy skyscrapers, indeed! This place *was* huge. Lots of tall buildings. He sure hoped he wouldn't have to jump any.

Melvin spent the day flying around the city, looking for a place to live.

He zoomed between the buildings, hovering a couple of times to flex his muscles and to smile at his reflection in the windows.

Then he flew out along the beach—

143 red bathing suits, 117 yellow bathing suits. "That's 260 bathing suits in all," Melvin said quickly.

Ah . . . math.

Later, while flying over the hillsides, he spotted it: an abandoned tree house on a hill overlooking the city.

"The perfect hideout for a superhero," Melvin said to himself.

In fact, it was the perfect place for any kid. It was set in an oak tree and had windows on every side. And a roof. Melvin had no idea if it ever rained in Los Angeles, but if it did he'd have more than his cape to keep himself dry.

He touched down on the rough boards of the tree house and began to set up his new home.

First on his list? Get a TV so he could watch cartoons. When superheroes aren't on the job, they're watching cartoons. Catch bad guys, watch cartoons. That's the superhero's day.

Second on Melvin's list was to stock up on snacks. Superheroes didn't eat regular meals. They snacked. Heavy meals made it hard to fly, and Melvin had enough trouble as it was. Besides, there was nothing in the code that said he had to eat vegetables. It was probably a good idea, but it wasn't in the code. And didn't the human body use whatever food it was given and turn it into energy—no matter what that food was? This made sense to Melvin.

Later that day, he sat in his tree house eating pretzels and drinking root beer and watching his favorite cartoon—*The Adventures of Thunderman.*

Thunderman had no problem stopping trains or leaping tall buildings.

When the cartoon was over, Melvin turned off the TV. He looked down at the city from his spot on the hill.

"Okay, bad guys, where are you?"

"JUST DOING MY JOB, MA'AM"

And then he heard it—a cry for help.

"Help! Stop, thief!"

Melvin threw himself out one of the windows of his tree house . . .

. . . and hit the ground. *Crash!*

"Gotta watch that first step," he said, getting to his feet. "Up, up, and away."

Once again, he was up and flying on his fifth try.

He zoomed down into the city with his cape flapping behind him. He scanned back and forth over the busy streets. Cars, buses, people. *Thank heavens*, thought Melvin, *everyone has on clean underwear.*

"Help! I'm being robbed!" A lady ran out of a store. "They're getting away!"

Two masked men with bags of money were getting into a car. *Good!* Melvin thought, *it's not a speeding locomotive.* He had no problem stopping cars.

He swooped from the sky, picked up the car, and dumped the bad guys onto the pavement. Before they could run

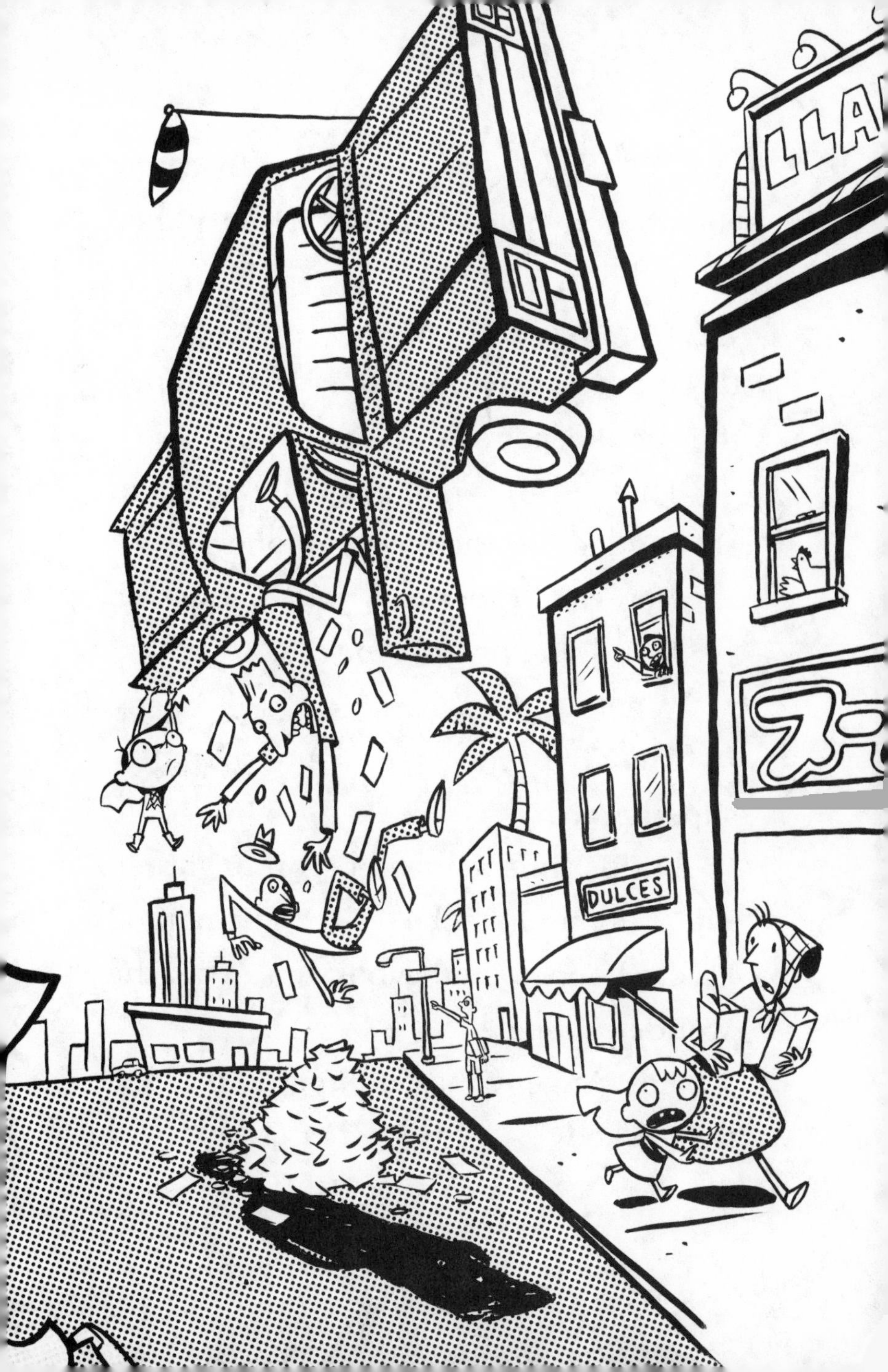
DULCES

away, Melvin grabbed them by their collars and held them until the police arrived.

"They took 581 dollars from register three and 833 dollars from register four," the shopkeeper said.

"That's 1,414 dollars," Melvin said. He handed her the bags of money.

"How can I ever thank you?" she asked.

"Just doing my job, ma'am."

"What's your name?"

"Melvin Beederman. I am your new superhero."

By this time a crowd began to gather. The butcher, the baker, a guy named Fred. Shoppers and cabdrivers. Milo the Wonder Tailor.

"Los Angeles has a superhero?" one man asked.

"We haven't had a superhero since Kareem Abdul-Jabbar retired," said another.

Milo the Wonder Tailor handed Melvin his card. "If you ever have a problem with your cape, call me. I'll fix it for free."

"Thanks," Melvin said.

Then he waited until everyone went back to their shops and their shopping before he headed back to the tree house. No one saw that it took him five tries to get up in the air.

Word spread quickly. The TV news guy announced, "Superhero Melvin, the first superhero in Los Angeles since you-know-who retired, foiled some would-be robbers today."

The newspaper headlines read, "There's a superhero in town. Welcome!"

Policemen talked about it. "Did you hear what Melvin Beederman did?"

And back at his tree house, Melvin looked down at the M on his chest and thought, *Maybe I* can *do this job after all.*

But later, as night came and Melvin sat doodling math problems on the dusty boards of the tree house, he began to miss his buddies back at the academy—Superhero Margaret and Superhero James. Now he was alone. Completely alone. He almost missed Superhero Carl.

Almost.

MEANWHILE...

While Melvin Beederman was busy becoming famous, Candace Brinkwater was on the verge of fame herself. She had tried out for the school play, and the director had just put up the notice of the actors and actresses who got parts.

Candace had tried out for many plays in the past. Once she was a tree, and another time she was a weed. Those were the kinds of parts Candace usually got—weeds and trees. She never got to *say* anything.

Everyone said she was the best weed they had ever seen.

So now Candace could not believe her eyes when she looked at the list of names.

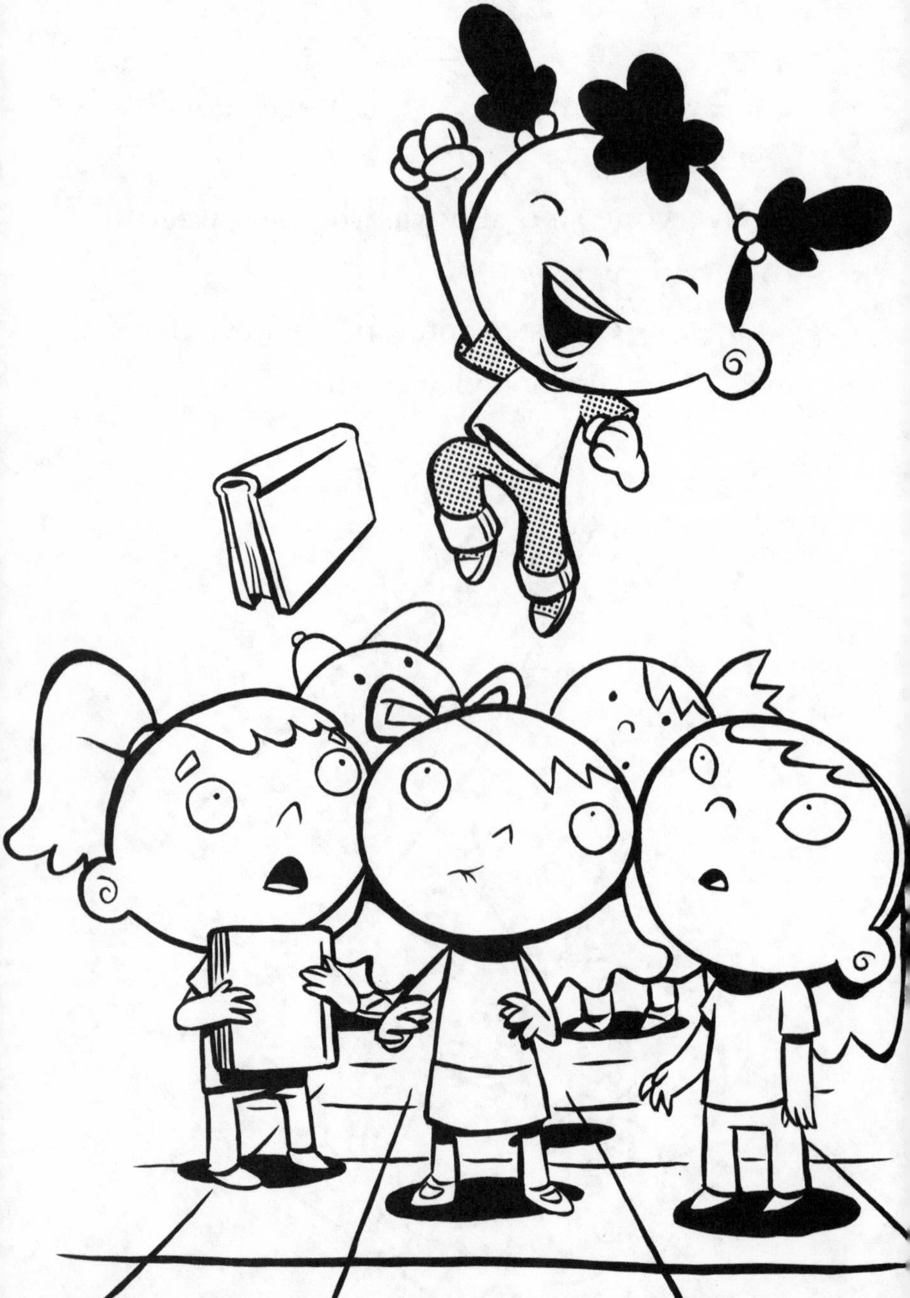

"I got the lead! I got the lead!" she said, jumping up and down.

She hugged all her friends. She even hugged a few enemies—Julia, Cathleen, a guy named Fred.

At home there was more celebrating.

Her mom hugged her.

Her sister slapped her a high-five.

Her dog Smedley licked her face.

Her dad held up his glass of root beer. "Here's to my little actress. I'm glad you're not a weed."

KNOW YOUR WEAKNESS

At the Superhero Academy they never came right out and told you what your weakness was. You found that out over the course of two years. If you discovered your weakness on your own, then you had to deal with it on your own. And that was part of the training.

Superhero Margaret became weak in the presence of jelly donuts. For Superhero James it was Ping-Pong balls.

Once, at a Ping-Pong championship, James fell to his knees, gasping, "Can't . . . move . . . get . . . me . . . out . . . of . . . here."

His classmates dragged him outside.

Melvin was the last one to learn his weakness. He and his classmates had been down at the railroad tracks all morning, stopping trains (they had taken a break from tall-building leaping). Afterward, as they were heading back to school, they passed a deli.

Melvin felt faint. His heart pounded and he had trouble breathing. He fell to his knees, gasping, "Can't . . . move . . . get . . . me . . . out . . . of . . . here."

His classmates carried him all the way back to school.

Problem was, Melvin still didn't know what his weakness was. It was something in the deli, but what?

Was it pastrami on rye?

Egg salad on white?

Tuna on wheat?

Perhaps it was the owner's aftershave.

Trial and error was the only way to find out. Back at the academy, Superhero James and Superhero Margaret did the testing, starting with all the lunch meats.

"How's this?" James asked, waving a piece of pastrami in front of Melvin's nose.

"Looks delicious," Melvin replied.

"How about this?" Margaret asked, holding a slice of turkey.

"Looks almost as delicious as that pastrami."

James and Margaret had everything that could possibly go in a sandwich laid out on a long table. One by one they went down the list.

"Ham?"

"Tasty."

"Bacon, lettuce, and tomato?"

"Yum."

Then James picked up a slice of bologna. "How about this?"

Melvin fell to his knees, gasping, "Can't . . . move . . . get . . . me . . . out . . . of . . . here."

They did.

Melvin had found his weakness. Bologna.

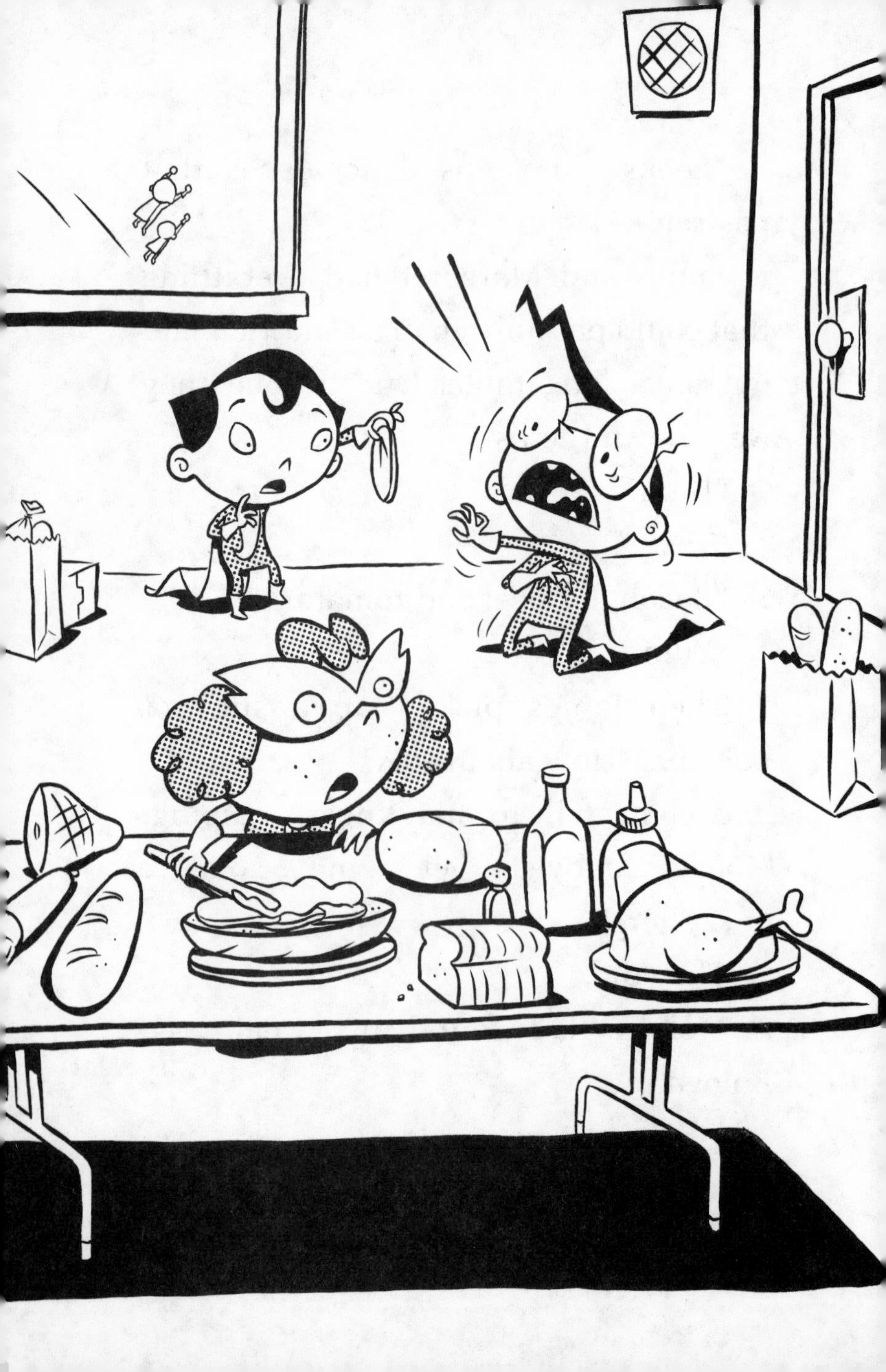

Back in Los Angeles, Melvin was busy. There were criminals all over the place. Muggers, robbers, a bad guy named Fred.

But so far, no one had tried to make a getaway by train. And no bad guys had hideouts in tall buildings.

Best of all, no one had robbed a deli.

Melvin was glad. He knew his weakness. He knew better than to go near the cold cuts section of the supermarket.

Still, he was dying for a pastrami sandwich.

SHOW UP JUST
IN THE NICK OF TIME

Melvin Beederman was getting the hang of things. The nights were lonely, but mostly he was feeling better about his superhero life.

He was catching bad guys right and left.

He was on the news every night (the news came on right after *The Adventures of Thunderman*).

Of course, seeing everyone's underwear was very annoying, but he knew he'd

learn to turn off his x-ray vision some-
day. Headmaster Spinner had said so.

One day Melvin stood at the window
of his hideout, looking down
at the city.

There were 103 very tall buildings and 228 medium tall buildings. "That's 331 buildings," Melvin said proudly.

And then he heard it.

"Where's my baby?!"

Melvin dove out the window.

Crash!

He really had to start watching that first step. "Up, up, and away." *Splat!*

Thud!

Kabonk!

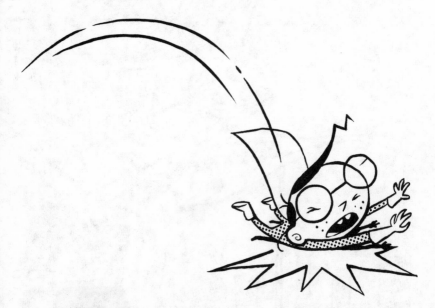

Once he was airborne, Melvin flew back and forth over the city.

"My baby! My baby!"

He looked and looked but couldn't see who was yelling.

"Someone help!"

And then he saw it: the fairgrounds, the tractor pull, lots of mud, screaming engines—and there in the middle of it all was a little boy, barely old enough to walk, saying, "Car, car."

"Help!" cried his mother. "Someone save my baby!"

Melvin swooped down over the race-track and snatched the boy just as he was about to get trampled by the tractors.

Mud flew about. Melvin used his cape to shield the boy.

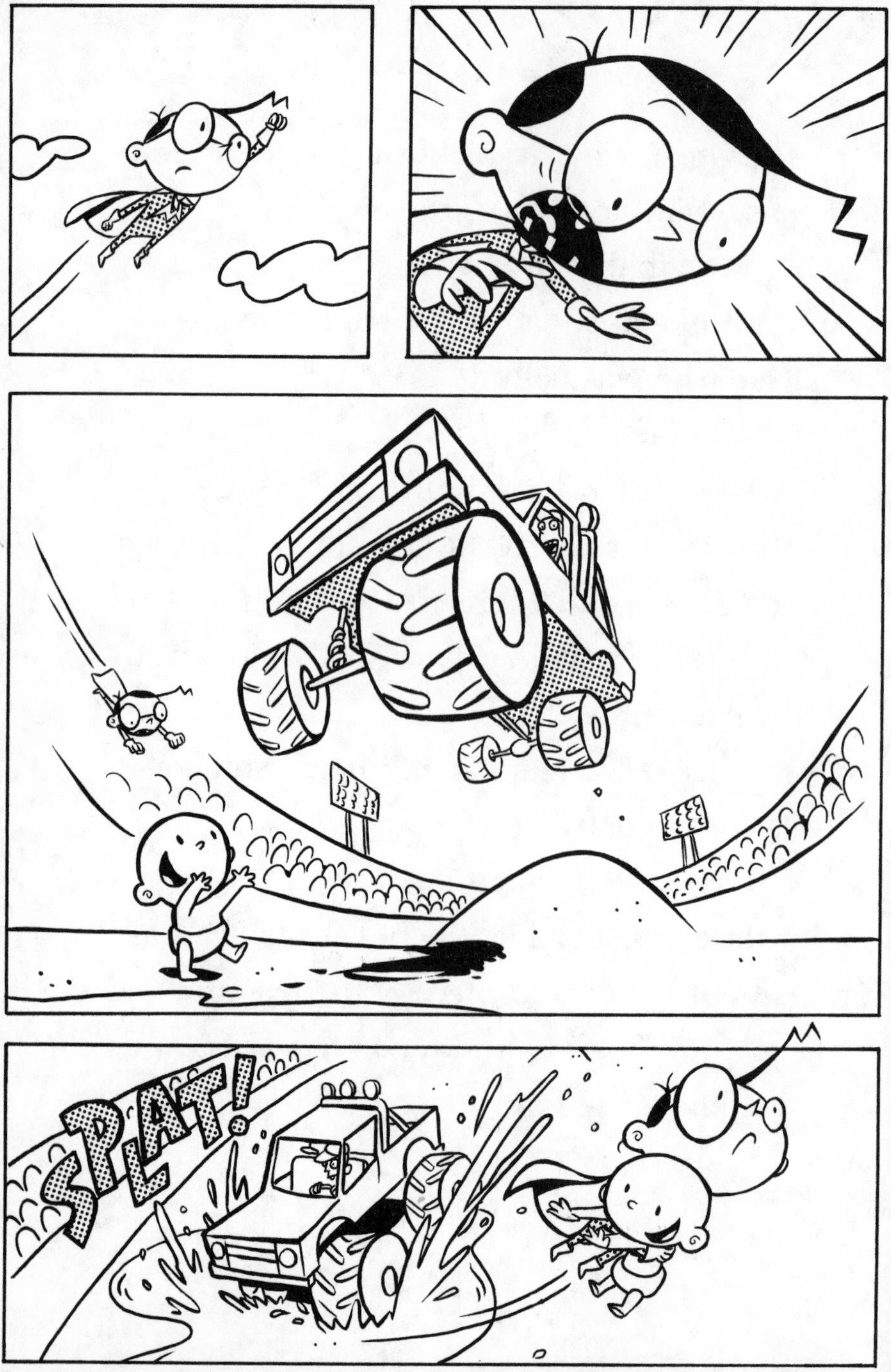
SPLAT!

The crowd cheered. It was the best show they had ever seen.

Melvin gave the child back to his mother.

"You saved him," she said with tears in her eyes.

"Just in the nick of time," Melvin said.

"How can I ever thank you?"

"Just doing my job, ma'am."

Then Melvin looked down at his muddy cape. It had to be against the code to have a cape that looked like that.

ALWAYS KEEP
YOUR CAPE CLEAN

Yes, it was against the code to have a
cape that looked like that.

The next day, Melvin took his cape to
the cleaners.

"How's the superhero business?" asked the man behind the counter.

"Busy," said Melvin.

"Your cape will be ready in three days."

"Three days! Holy vacation!"

Holy vacation, indeed! Melvin knew he couldn't fly without his cape. Not even in six tries. And so he walked home. Melvin Beederman had to take a break from catching bad guys.

This was bad news for everyone in Los Angeles, because right then the McNasty Brothers broke out of jail. Filthy McNasty and his brother, Grunge, to be exact. Those notorious bank robbers and all-around bad guys. They started robbing banks all over the city.

Everyone was crying for help.

"Superhero Melvin, we need you," said the chief of police.

"Superhero Melvin, where are you?" asked the mayor.

Holy ninety-eight-pound weakling!

thought Melvin. *This is terrible*. He could do nothing without his cape. And he wouldn't get it back from the cleaners for three days!

Holy ninety-eight pound weakling, indeed! This *was* terrible. He couldn't fly. He couldn't even see through walls.

And the McNasty Brothers, those notorious bank robbers and all-around bad guys, robbed bank after bank after bank.

"Superhero Melvin!" everyone yelled.

It was a cry for help, but Melvin Beederman had to say no. For the first time in his life he broke the code.

THE CAPELESS CRUSADER

Everyone was still screaming for help three days later when Melvin went to the cleaners for his cape. The McNasty Brothers were still robbing banks all over Los Angeles. Nobody could stop them.

At the cleaners, Melvin looked at his cape.

"Nice and clean," said the man behind the counter.

Melvin held it up. "What happened to it?"

"Must have shrunk."

It sure had. Superhero Melvin's cape was half its original size.

"No use crying over shrunk cape," said the man behind the counter. "Go catch bad guys, Melvin Beederman. Go get those McNasty Brothers."

Melvin took his cape and left. He had to catch those McNasty Brothers. Besides, a cape was a cape, no matter what size. A superhero was a superhero. And his town needed him.

He went behind the store and put on the extra-small cape. He didn't want anyone to count how many times it took him to get up and flying.

"Up, up, and away."

Crash!

"Up, up, and away."

Splat!

Melvin didn't worry about it until he had tried to get off the ground six times. Then his sixth try came and went, and he started worrying.

Seven. *Thud!*

Eight. *Kabonk!*

No matter how many times he tried, Melvin couldn't get up in the air.

Twenty-nine. *Crash!*

Thirty. *Splat!*

It was no use. Melvin couldn't fly.

"Superhero Melvin, where are you?" Everyone was crying for help. And Filthy McNasty and his brother, Grunge, kept robbing banks.

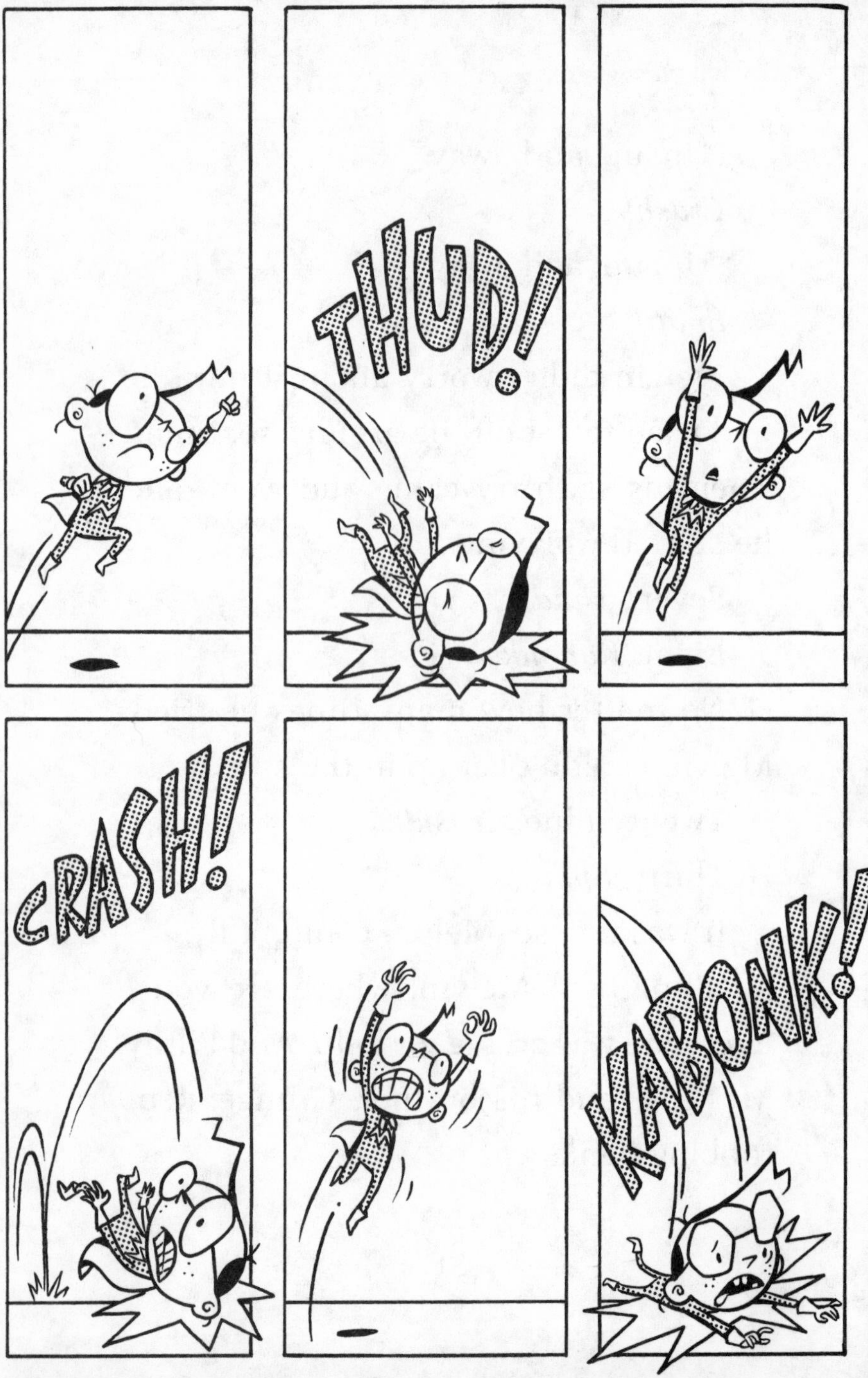
THUD!
CRASH!
KABONK!

MEANWHILE . . .

While Superhero Melvin was busy losing his superpowers, Candace Brinkwater was busy getting ready for her school play.

"Did you finish your homework?" her mother asked, helping her daughter get dressed.

"I hate word problems," Candace said. Boy, did she. The only thing worse than word problems was vegetables.

"You can finish your math when you get home from the play." Mrs. Brinkwater was as excited as Candace about the play, but that didn't mean she would let her daughter neglect her studies.

Candace would almost rather eat vegetables. Almost.

"What on earth happened to your cape?" her mother asked suddenly, holding it up. She put the cape on Candace. It was so long that it dragged on the floor.

"Something must have happened to it at the cleaners," Candace said. "Maybe Milo can fix it."

"We don't have time for Milo the Wonder Tailor."

This was a problem. Who ever heard of Little Red Riding Hood dragging her cape in the dirt? If there was a code for little girls in red capes, Candace would be breaking it for sure.

But as her mother said, they had no time to fix it. And as they say, the show must go on. It did.

When Candace stepped onto the stage that night, dragging her long cape behind her, the crowd roared with laughter—teachers, parents, the sound man named Fred.

Candace tripped over the cape many times during the play. This just caused more laughter.

Later, when she got to Grandmother's house, she knocked on the door so hard that the house began to fall down. Candace rushed in, grabbed the wolf and her tied-up grandmother, and carried them to safety as the house crashed to the floor.

The crowd cheered.

"What a finale!"

"She's the best Little Red Riding Hood I've ever seen."

"And the strongest."

"She'll never play a weed again."

Candace held Grandmother and the wolf, and looked out at the crowd. She loved the cheers. She loved the applause.

Only one thing bothered her: Why was everyone in their underwear?

UNSUPERHERO CARL

While Melvin Beederman was busy losing his superpowers and Candace Brinkwater was busy rescuing wolves and tied-up grandmothers, Superhero Carl was behaving very unsuperhero-ish.

People vacationing in Fiji were being robbed.

A lady's purse was snatched from right under her nose. A kid's skateboard was grabbed from right under his feet!

"Somebody help!" they yelled.

A cry for help. The code did say "Never say no to a cry for help." But Superhero Carl was too busy to bother.

Now that Headmaster Spinner wasn't watching, Carl didn't care about the code. He spent his time in his hotel room on the beach and worked on his Web site.

Outside his window someone ran by with a purse and a skateboard. Carl did nothing about it.

He typed on his computer. "Melvin Beederman," he sneered, "you're about to have a very bad day."

SLOWER THAN
A SPEEDING BULLET

Melvin Beederman was having more than a bad day. He was having bad *days*. After trying to get off the ground 642 times—*Crash! Splat! Thud! Kabonk!*—he returned to his tree house.

He looked at himself in his full-length mirror. He was bruised and grass stained. Worse than that, he looked ridiculous in his tiny cape. "*Holy I-look-like-poop!*" he said to himself. "*This is bad news.*"

Holy he-looks-like-poop,
indeed! This was bad news.

What to do? He wandered
around the tree house thinking.
Then he got an
idea. Maybe he
couldn't fly, but
he could still run.
Melvin dusted
himself off, cleaned
up his bruises, and
set off for the track at
the local college. He
remembered a time when he was as
fast as a speeding bullet. He had to test
himself.

"Mind if I run a few with you boys?"
he asked, stepping up to the starting line
of the hundred-yard dash.

The runners looked up.

"Look, it's Superhero Melvin!"

"Oh, no, we'll lose for sure. He's fast as a speeding bullet."

"What happened to your cape?"

"Haven't you heard of Milo the Wonder Tailor?"

Melvin ignored the questions.

The coach said, "On your mark. Get set. Go!"

Melvin Beederman finished last.

The runners cheered. It was the first time any of them had beaten a superhero.

"Let's go catch bad guys," one of them said. If they could outrun Melvin Beederman, they could certainly catch bad guys.

Next Melvin went to the local high school. These guys were younger.

"Mind if I run a few with you boys?" he asked.

"Hey, it's Superhero Melvin!"

"What happened to your cape?"

Melvin shrugged and stepped up to the starting line. Someone whispered, "I hear he's fast as a speeding bullet."

The coach pointed a pistol in the air. "On your mark. Get set." *Bang!*

Melvin Beederman finished last.

There was only one thing to do: Try his luck at the junior high.

These guys were even smaller. And younger. Shorter legs.

He couldn't possibly finish last here. Melvin puffed out his chest. "Mind if I run a few with you boys?" he asked in his deepest voice.

"What happened to your—"

"It shrank, okay?" Melvin said. He was already ashamed of his tiny cape. Did they have to keep asking about it?

He stepped up to the starting line.

The coach said, "On your mark. Get set. Go!"

Once again, last place. "Holy slow poke! This is horrible!" Melvin said.

Holy slow poke, indeed! Horrible, horrible, horrible.

All the children wanted to go catch bad guys.

Melvin thought of trying his luck at the local elementary school, but what if he lost again . . . to a bunch of third-graders? Some things were just too depressing. So instead, he went home. Back to the tree house to think things over.

That night he watched *The Adventures of Thunderman*. Thunderman was so busy catching bad guys that he hired an assistant to help him. Her name was Thunder Thighs.

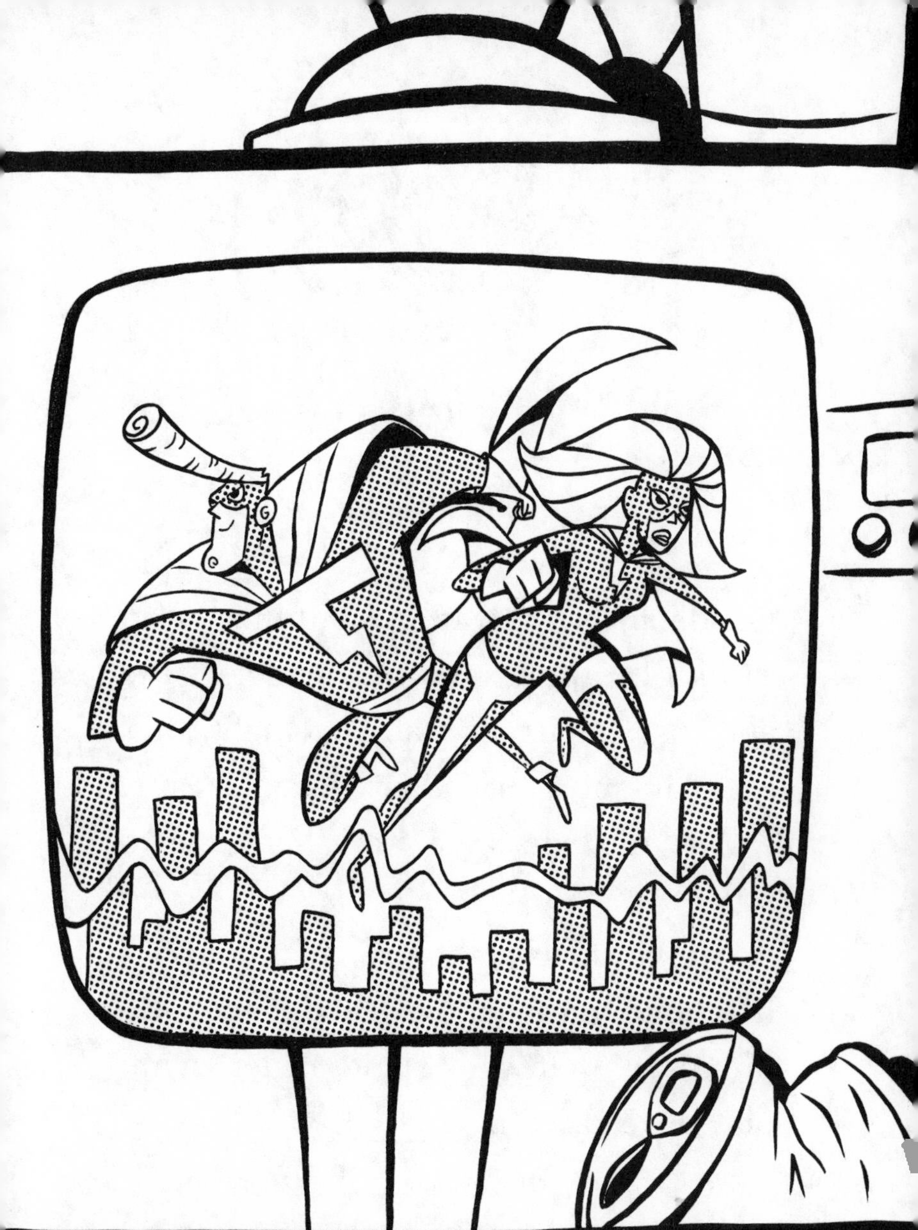

MEANWHILE . . .

Candace Brinkwater couldn't stop thinking about it: the cheers, the applause, the underwear. That night, after the play, she slept in her oversized cape.

The next day, she wore her cape to school.

Mr. Crimshaw, the principal, told her how much he enjoyed the show. He promised that she would never again play a weed.

"Thanks, Mr. Crimshaw," she said, then whispered to herself, "Nice boxers."

At recess Candace decided to join in a game of kickball. When it was her turn at the plate, the other kids made fun of her.

"Look, it's Little Red Riding Hood."

"Easy out."

"Move in, everybody."

Candace had never been great at sports. She was the only kid to strike out in kickball nine times in a row.

But now, here came the pitch. . . .

Candace reared back and kicked with everything she had. The ball sailed over the school. A home run! Candace's team won the game. And nobody saw that ball again.

The players on the other team couldn't believe their eyes. They watched with their mouths hanging open as Candace rounded the bases.

She did a victory dance on home plate with the rest of her team.

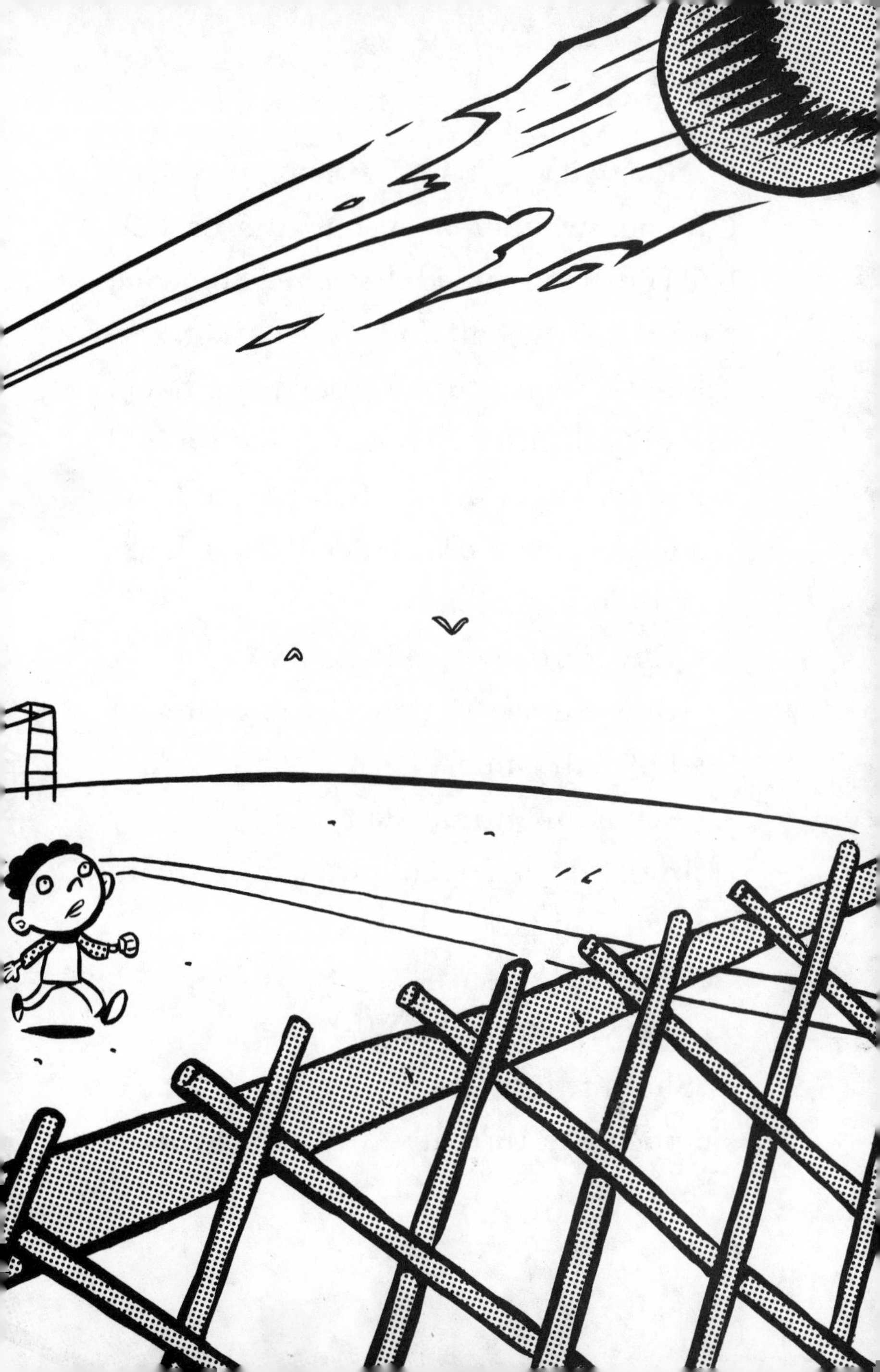

Now, with no ball, the game was over. Candace wandered over to the basket-ball court and joined the game. Someone passed her the ball under the basket, and Candace slammed it through the hoop. The only third-grader ever to slam-dunk!

"Holy sports-hero!" Candace said.

Holy sports-hero, indeed! First kick-ball, then basketball.

Word spread quickly.

"Did you see Candace Brinkwater in the kickball game?"

"What about that slam-dunk?"

In the days that followed, every team wanted Candace.

"We get Candace."

"No, you don't. We do."

She hit the tetherball so hard that it snapped the rope like it was spaghetti.

More kick balls disappeared over the school, never to be seen again. She scored 500 points in a single basketball game. All dunks.

The boys were very impressed with her one-arm push-ups.

"Eighty-two, eighty-three . . ."

"Go, Candace, go!"

But that was only the beginning. One day she was in class, working on a nasty word problem (she still hated math), when she heard something. Whispers.

"Shh . . . quiet now."

She looked at her classmates. They were all busy with math.

She went back to her word problem. Then she heard it again.

"Got it. Let's go." She heard footsteps. What was going on? Change jingled.

Candace jumped up. "Somebody's stealing the milk money!"

She dashed out of the room and down the hall, her extra-long cape flying behind her. Two sixth-graders were coming out of the office with their pockets bulging.

She grabbed them by their collars and held them until Principal Crimshaw got there.

"Thank you, Candace," he said.

Candace smiled. She felt like telling him she was just doing her job.

Word got around that not only could Candace Brinkwater slam-dunk and break the tetherball rope, but you had better behave around her, too. She'd started showing up just in the nick of time to save little kids from being pounded on by big kids.

It didn't take long for bullies to start tipping their ball caps when they passed her in the hall. "Good morning, Miss Brinkwater."

No one had ever called her Miss Brinkwater before.

By the end of the week she was flying.

This happened by accident. It was at the all-school track meet. Candace never liked sports of any kind, and she liked running least of all. But lately that had all changed. She felt strong, light on her feet. Something inside her told her she was as fast as a speeding bullet.

She stepped up to the starting line of the hundred-yard dash.

Principal Crimshaw pointed a pistol in the air. "On your mark, get set." *Bang!*

Candace zoomed down the track in world-record time: just three and a half seconds. She leaped for joy, and then . . . she just kept going up. She flew around the school yard. Everyone cheered.

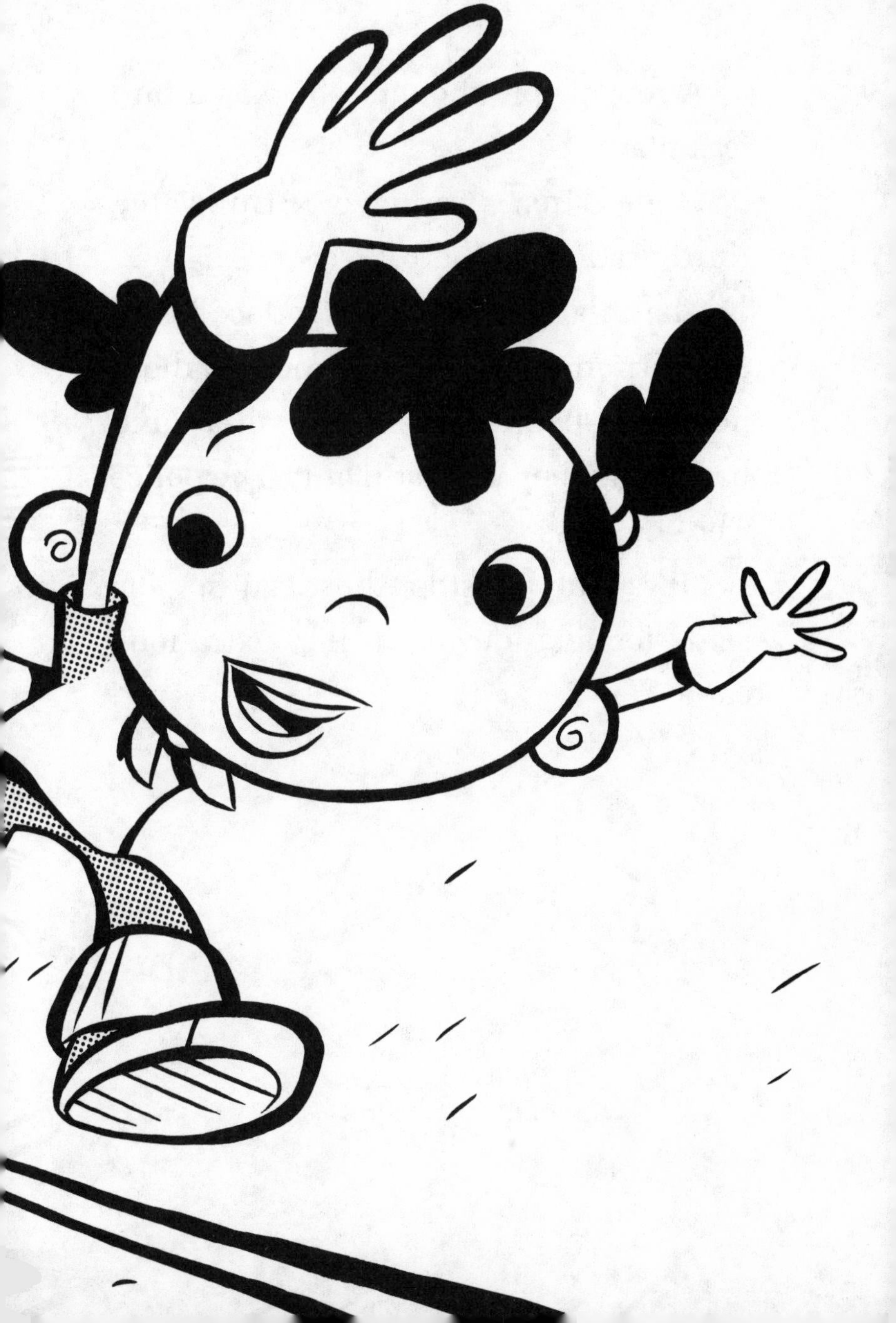

A few people thought she was a bird or a plane.

Nope. Just Candace Brinkwater, third-grade superhero.

That night on the TV, Candace heard a report on the McNasty Brothers, those notorious bank robbers and all-around bad guys. They were still at it. The police were helpless.

"It's time to stop those guys," she said, looking down at her extra-long cape.

PARTNERS IN UNCRIME

All Melvin's powers were gone. He
couldn't fly, couldn't run. True, he hadn't
seen anyone's underwear in days, but now
he almost missed even that.

Almost.

He was no longer Superhero Melvin.
He was just plain old Melvin Beederman.
And now that he was 3,000 miles away
from his friends at the academy,
he was more alone than ever.

79

He searched his memory. What did the code say about losing your powers?

It didn't say anything. He was completely on his own. Not even the code could help.

Melvin wandered around his tree house thinking.

"Maybe I can start with something easy," he said to himself. It was all he could think of. Start simple and work up.

Maybe he could rescue a cat from a tree or help an old lady across the street. Before long he would be catching bad guys again.

Maybe.

Melvin climbed down from the tree house. He was careful not to jump. Then he went into town.

The streets were crowded—shoppers, storekeepers, a garbage man named Fred. Melvin looked up at the tall buildings. A couple of people saw his small cape and told him about Milo the Wonder Tailor.

And then he heard it.

"Stop! Thief!"

Melvin saw a man running, holding a lady's purse.

"Stop that purse snatcher!"

Melvin ran after him. He was nowhere near as fast as a speeding bullet. But it was a cry for help, and the code must be followed.

Melvin ran as fast as he could.

Then a flash of red zoomed past him, heading in the same direction. When Melvin arrived at the corner, breathing hard, he saw a little girl with an over-sized cape hanging on to the purse snatcher and smiling. The police showed up a few moments later and took the bad guy away.

Melvin would recognize that cape anywhere.

"That . . . *gasp* . . . is . . . *gasp* . . . my cape," he said, out of breath. He took off his mini one and handed it to her. "I think this one is yours."

This made perfect sense. Candace's cape dragged on the ground, while Melvin's was way too short.

But instead of being happy, all Candace could think about was the kickball game, the basketball game, catching the milk money thieves . . . and now a purse snatcher. What about the McNastys? Weren't they next on her list?

"But I really like being a superhero," she said, taking off her cape.

"I like it more," Melvin said. He put on his cape and walked away. Suddenly, everywhere he looked—underwear. He was back to normal.

"But, but, but . . . ," the girl pleaded as Melvin kept walking.

Halfway down the block he stopped and turned. *Wait a minute,* he thought. *Even Thunderman had a superhero assistant.*

He had an idea.

That night Milo the Wonder Tailor worked late. He took Melvin Beederman's cape and made it into *two* capes. He even added a little material so that it still reached down to Melvin's ankles. And now Candace's cape no longer dragged on the ground.

And for the first time in history, Los Angeles, California, had two super-heroes at the same time.

"Teammates?" Melvin said to Candace.

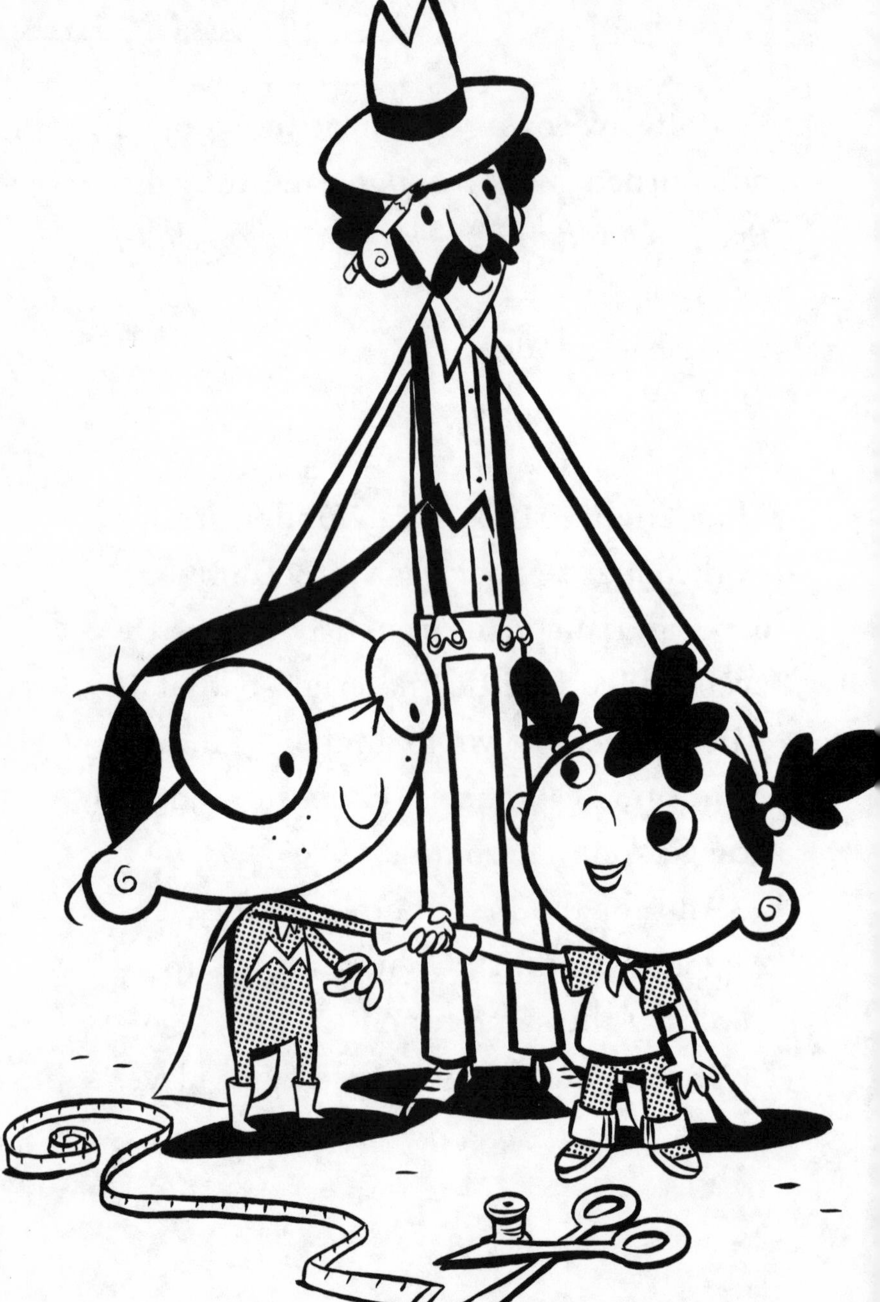

"Teammates," Candace replied.

"Let's go get those McNasty Brothers. Up, up, and away."

Candace was up and flying on the first try . . . but not Melvin. . . .

Crash!

"Be with you in a moment," he said, brushing himself off.

Splat!

Thud!

Kabonk!

Some things never changed.

THE McNASTYS

All the McNastys smelled bad. It had been part of their family history for centuries. And it was still going STRONG.

Mr. McNasty smelled bad. Mrs. McNasty smelled bad. Even their gold-fish smelled bad. If you ever see extra bubbles in their fish tank, you'd better run and not look back.

So Filthy McNasty and his brother,

Grunge, had a lot to live up to. And they did. They smelled worst of all. But this didn't mean they were stupid.

Stinky, yes. Stupid, no.

Their lair was on the fifty-third floor of Grunion/Fig Building in the city. Not hideout—lair.

"Get away from that window," Grunge told his brother. Everybody thought Filthy was the leader of the gang. But really it was Grunge. He passed gas more often, too.

"Don't worry," Filthy said. "Superhero Melvin can't leap tall buildings, haven't you heard? And I hear he lost a race to a bunch of junior high kids."

"Yeah, I hear he's been having very bad days. He hasn't been showing up just in the nick of time for anything. But get away from that window anyway. You can't trust superheroes."

This was actually one of the laws of bad guys. Bad guys didn't have a code, but they did have laws. Rules of thumb. For example, rule number one was "Be nasty at all times." Rule number two was "Don't trust superheroes." You could get pretty far as a bad guy with those two rules alone.

"Don't worry," Filthy said. He pointed to the computer on the desk. "We know everything we need to about Melvin Beederman."

Grunge was busy counting their loot.

Not money—loot. If you withdraw cash from a bank, it's called money. If you steal it, it's called loot. And the McNastys had a lot of it.

"I don't know if I trust the Unofficial Melvin Beederman Web Site," Grunge said.

"You worry too much, Grunge. Whew! What's that nasty smell?"

"Hey, I'm a McNasty and proud of it," Grunge said as Filthy fanned the air. Grunge had always been big on family, even his smelly one. Yes, the McNasty family traditions were still going STRONG!

"Now for the last time, get away from that window."

Filthy did what his brother told him. Deep down he knew they didn't have to worry. They were on the fifty-third floor, after all, and Melvin had a hard time getting up in the air. But just in case, Filthy had a secret weapon. "Melvin Beederman doesn't have a chance," he said to himself.

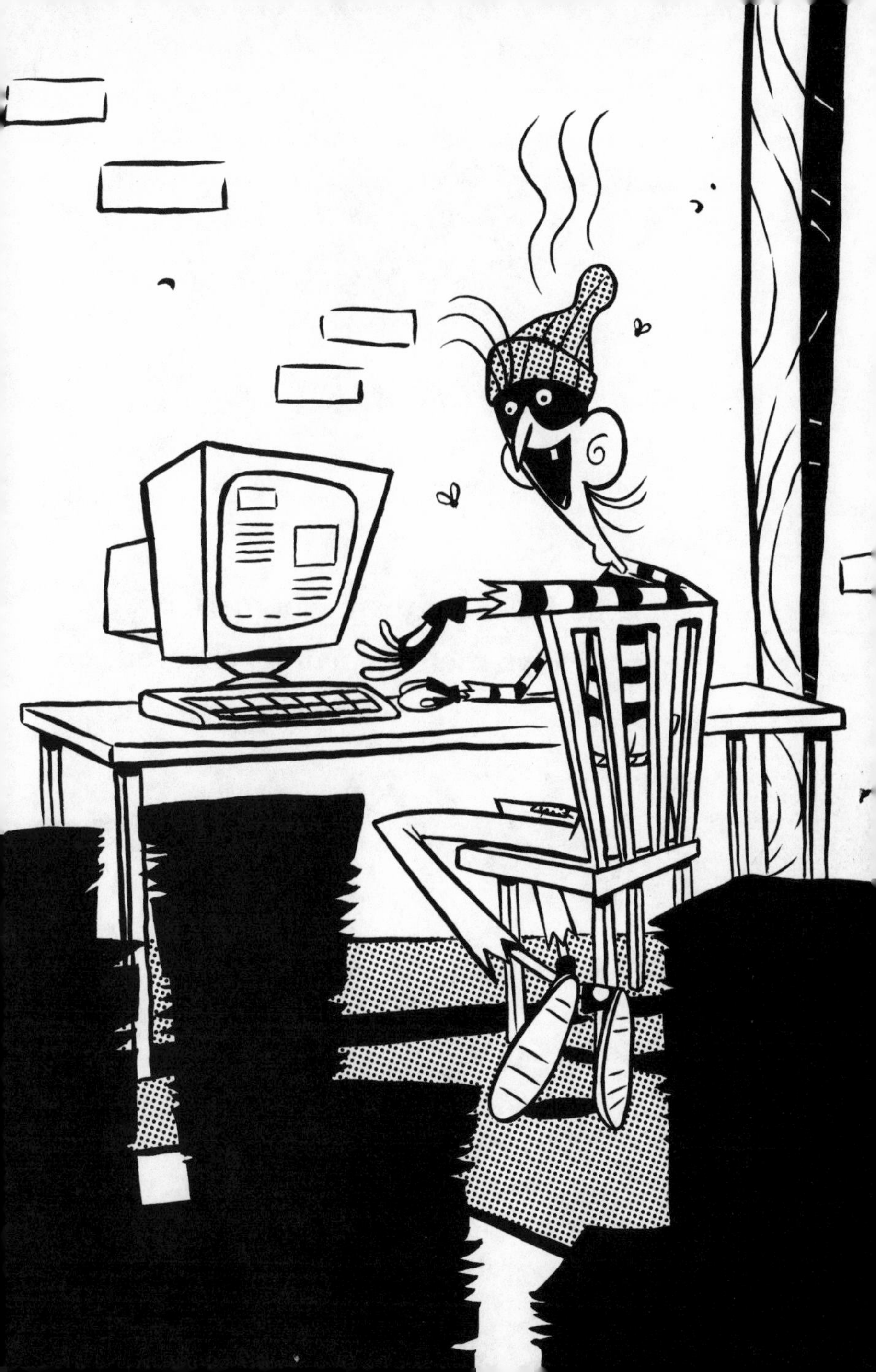

15

"NOT SO FAST!"

The crime-fighting team zoomed over
the city. Down below, people cheered.
Window cleaners, schoolchildren, a traffic
cop named Fred.

Superhero Melvin was back on the job, and this time he had a superhero assistant.

Melvin and Candace flew to the police station, hovered in front of the chief's window, and saluted. Then they did the same outside the mayor's window.

But now how to find the McNastys?

They flew between very tall buildings and medium tall ones. Out to the beach. Up over the hillsides. Melvin pointed out his home.

"You live in a tree house?" Candace asked.

"Yep."

"You're so lucky."

Back and forth they flew. Around the airport, over the harbor.

Then they smelled something.

"What is that nasty smell?" Candace asked.

"You mean, what is that *Mc*Nasty smell?" Melvin said.

They looked at each other. "The McNasty Brothers!"

Nobody but the McNastys could smell that bad. Melvin and Candace were downtown among the tall buildings, and they put their superhero noses to work. They sniffed around. Here a sniff, there a sniff, everywhere a sniff sniff.

"Who said that?" Candace asked.

"Who said what?"

"Who said 'sniff sniff'?"

"The narrator. Ignore him. We have a job to do."

The stink was coming from the Grunion/Fig Building, of course. "They're in there," Melvin said. His nose was never wrong. Not only could he *see* through walls but he could *smell* through them, too.

"Are you sure?" Candace asked. "Maybe it's a dead elephant."

"You take the upper floors. I'll search the lower ones," Melvin commanded. He was the crime-fighting team leader. After all, he had graduated from the academy, while Candace had merely caught milk money thieves and a purse snatcher.

Candace zoomed skyward. Melvin started on the ground floor and worked his way up.

The building was deserted. Melvin moved down the dark hallways, kicking in doors and saying "Aha!" only to find the rooms empty. No sign of the McNasty Brothers. No sign of those notorious bank robbers and all-around bad guys.

They have to be here, Melvin thought. That smell. It had to be Filthy and Grunge.

Melvin kept moving, kept kicking in doors.

And then he heard something, very faint, from one of the upper floors.

"Can't . . . move . . . get . . . me . . . out . . . of . . . here."

Candace was in trouble!

Melvin raced down the hallway and

crashed through the window. Up and flying on the first try! He zoomed skyward, circling the building, scanning for his partner.

"Can't . . . move . . . get . . . me . . . out . . . of . . . here."

He crashed through the window on the fifty-third floor, then crept down the hall. He stopped when he heard voices and laughter. He put his ear to a door and listened.

"Having a little trouble, girlie? Where's your pal, Melvin Beederman? We have a surprise for him."

Melvin kicked down the door. "Not so fast!" he said.

There stood Filthy McNasty and his brother, Grunge. Why were they smiling?

Candace was tied to a post, hands behind her back. Melvin moved forward. And then he saw it. . . .

There was a bologna sandwich in front of her on the floor.

He fell to his knees, gasping, "Can't . . . move . . . get . . . me . . . out . . . of . . . here."

"Tie him up, Filthy," Grunge ordered.

When Melvin was tied to the post, back-to-back with Candace, Grunge said, "Well, well, the famous Melvin Beederman. We know all about you from your Web site. Everything you'd ever want to know about Superhero Melvin . . . tall buildings, trains." He pointed to the bologna sandwich. "And of course your weakness around a certain lunch meat."

"I don't have a Web site," Melvin said.

Filthy pointed to the computer. "Yes, you do. Created someplace south of here, if I remember correctly. The Fiji Islands."

Carl! Melvin thought. It had to be Superhero Carl.

He struggled to get loose, but he had no strength. He tried to remember what the code said. But there was nothing. It was the one thing they didn't teach at the academy—what to do in the face of your weakness.

Grunge said, "Here's an interesting bit of news. They're knocking this building down next week."

Melvin and Candace stared at him.

"Yep, it's true. A week from now this will be a pile of rubble. The world will never know what happened to Melvin Beederman and his superhero assistant."

"Her name is Candace," Melvin said.

"Whatever. Grab the loot, Filthy. Time to make our getaway."

"What do we do?" Candace asked when they were alone. She pulled against the ropes, struggling to get free.

The only thing going through Melvin's head was *Can't . . . move . . . get . . . me . . . out . . . of . . . here.*

He needed a plan.

YOUR BRAIN IS YOUR
GREATEST WEAPON

Noggin power. It was their only way out.
Melvin had no strength to break the
ropes that tied him to the post. He had
to use his brain.

"What are we going to do?" Candace
asked again. She had no experience with
this kind of stuff. She'd only caught a
couple of milk money thieves and a purse
snatcher. It was her first time up against
notorious bank robbers and all-around

bad guys. Besides, noggin power wasn't her thing. She hated word problems.

"*Think*," Melvin said to himself.

Before them sat a foot-long bologna sandwich. Melvin grew weaker just looking at it. *There must be a way out of this*, he thought. The academy expected him to find the answer. *Think, Melvin Beederman.*

He stared hard at the sandwich. And suddenly it came to him.

Of course! Bologna was food. If he ate it and his body digested it, wouldn't it no longer be a bologna sandwich? Didn't the body convert all food into energy? And if it was no longer a bologna sandwich, couldn't he snap the ropes like they were spaghetti?

"I think I know a way out of this," Melvin said to Candace.

"How?" Candace asked.

"We can eat the sandwich."

"Are you crazy?"

"Trust me," Melvin said. "I graduated at the top of my class. If we eat the sandwich it won't be able to hurt us. It will no longer exist."

One thing he didn't tell her: It could also kill them. Something that made them that weak on the outside might do even more damage if it was on the inside.

But they had to take the chance.

"It's our only way out, Candace. This building is being knocked down soon. The McNastys were right. No one will ever know what happened to us. We can sit and wait to die, or we can do something about it."

Candace nodded. She had hated bologna even before she was a superhero, but it was the only way. "Let's do it," she said.

It wasn't easy with their hands tied. But they did it—they ate the bologna sandwich.

Then they fainted.

"Are you okay, Melvin?" Candace asked sometime later.

Melvin slowly sat up. He blinked a few times. "We're alive! How do you feel, Candace?"

"I'll tell you in a second." She snapped the ropes and stood up. "Great! I feel almost good enough to do math. Almost."

Melvin snapped his ropes and got to his feet. The plan had worked. The digested bologna didn't kill them or even

sap their strength. If anything, Melvin felt stronger than ever.

As a test he karate-chopped the post they had been tied to. It splintered.

"Time to catch those McNastys," Melvin said.

"Those notorious bank robbers and all-around bad guys," Candace added, kicking out one of the windows. "After you, boss."

"If you don't mind, I think I'll take the stairs," Melvin said. He had been up and flying on the first try when Candace was in trouble. Now that she was safe, he didn't want to risk jumping from the fifty-third floor. That first step might be more than even a superhero could handle.

Once on the ground floor, he launched himself.

Crash!

Splat!

Thud!

Kabonk!

Melvin Beederman was back to his old self. He smiled, glad to be alive, glad to be out in the fresh air once again.

"Any idea where the McNastys are?" Candace asked when he finally joined her in the air.

Melvin nodded. "I know exactly how they plan to get away." He banked right. "Follow me."

Candace did.

They flew past the police station and city hall but didn't stop to salute.

"Where are we going?" Candace asked.

Melvin pointed to a train pulling out of the station. "Have you ever stopped a speeding train, Candace?"

BELIEVE IN YOURSELF
AT ALL TIMES

"Are you sure they're on board?" Candace asked. She looked down at a train heading east out of Los Angeles.

"Yes, I'm sure." Superhero Carl had blabbed everything about Melvin to the world. Tall buildings, bologna, trains. Filthy McNasty had said so. "They'll be leaving by train. No question about it. Use your x-ray vision. I know they're on there somewhere."

By now the train was speeding down the track. The two superheroes stayed with it. They flew overhead, scanning for the McNasty Brothers. Those notorious bank robbers and all-around bad guys.

Then . . .

"What is that nasty smell?" Candace asked.

"You mean that *Mc*Nasty smell," Melvin said. He pointed to the middle car of the train. With their x-ray vision they saw through the metal roof. "There they are! Time to go to work, partner."

Filthy McNasty and his brother had on dark sunglasses and fake mustaches, but Melvin would know them anywhere.

"Right, partner." Candace had never in her life stopped a speeding train. She could slam-dunk, though. And she could run the hundred-yard dash in three and a half seconds.

Melvin had stopped a few trains, but it was never easy. His classmates at the academy had always laughed at him, especially Carl.

But now the whole city of Los Angeles was counting on him. He had to leave his past behind. He had to believe in himself.

"Follow me," he said.

Melvin and Candace zoomed to the front of the train. Then they dropped to the tracks and grabbed hold of the lead engine. Melvin placed his feet on one track, Candace put hers on the other. They leaned and pushed.

The train kept going.

"Push!" Melvin grunted. He looked behind him. The train was headed for a tunnel. They had to stop it before it got there. Once in the dark, the McNasty Brothers could get away. "Push!"

The two superheroes pushed against the train with all their might. Their feet smoked as they slid along the tracks. The tunnel was coming up. "Push!"

At last the train slowed. Finally it came to a stop.

Melvin slapped Candace a high-five. "Now that's what I call teamwork!"

But their job was not over.

Filthy McNasty and his brother, Grunge, jumped out the window of the middle car and ran, dragging their loot with them. Not money—loot.

"Stay here, Candace," Melvin said. "I'll get them. I used to be fast as a speeding bullet."

Melvin needed to do this alone. He had to find out if he could. He could fly again, but could he run? Hadn't he lost in a race to a bunch of junior high kids?

He took off after the McNasty Brothers, arms and legs pumping hard.

Yep. Fast as a speeding bullet. Maybe faster.

"Stop right there," he said, grabbing Filthy and Grunge by the collars.

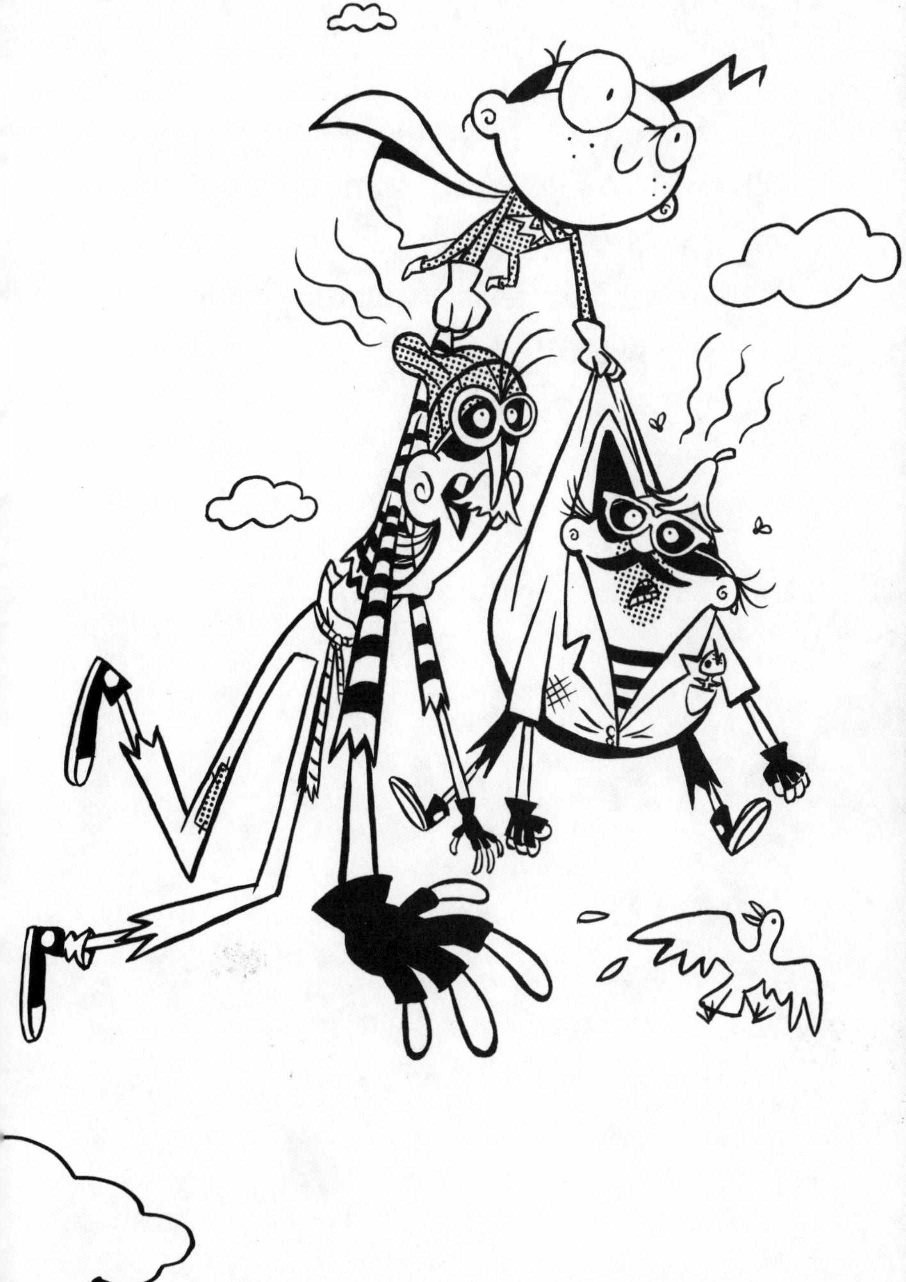

"How'd you get away?" Grunge yelled. "How'd you get away from that bologna sandwich?"

Melvin smiled. "Noggin power. My most powerful weapon."

NEVER BREAK UP
A GOOD TEAM

The mayor gave a huge party for Melvin and Candace. After all, Los Angeles had not had a superhero since you-know-who retired. And now they had two, a superhero team. Best of all, the McNasty Brothers, those notorious bank robbers and all-around bad guys, were back in prison.

Melvin and Candace shook hands with the mayor and the chief of police.

They had their pictures taken with a Girl Scout troop, and they signed lots of autographs.

Mostly they nibbled on pretzels and sipped root beer. This was Candace's favorite snack, too. She could not stand math, but at least she knew how to eat.

"You're the second-best superhero I've ever seen," Melvin told her.

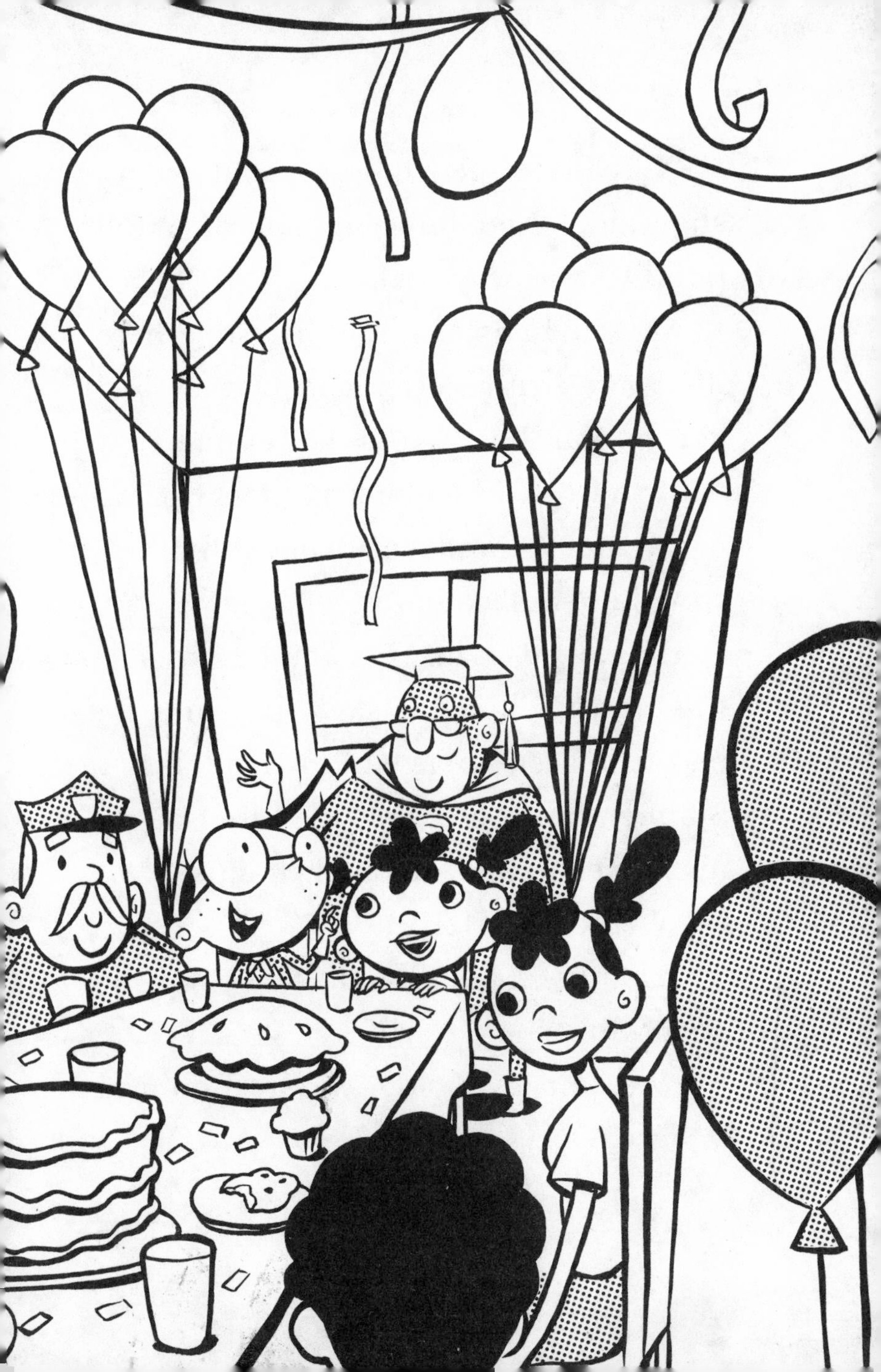

"I really liked stopping that train," she said. "And jumping out of a tall building was way cool."

Melvin had to admit his superhero life was getting better and better. He'd gotten off the ground in one try. And now he was no longer alone. He had a partner—Candace Brinkwater, his superhero assistant.

He looked at all the smiling faces at the party. Then he saw someone he had not seen in a while: Headmaster Spinner, from the academy, who walked up to Melvin and shook his hand.

"Well done, Melvin."

"Thanks," Melvin said. "Did you hear about Superhero Carl?"

"Yes, and I've taken care of him and

his Web site. That's why I'm here. I told you if you did well here, you could have your pick of assignments. It seems we have an opening in Fiji."

Melvin looked at Candace, then back to Headmaster Spinner.

"Think about it, Melvin," Headmaster Spinner said. "Sunshine, coral reefs . . ."

"Thanks," Melvin said, "but I'm part of a team now. Headmaster Spinner, meet Candace Brinkwater, my partner in uncrime."

Candace shook the headmaster's hand.

"This town needs us," Melvin went on. But deep down he knew it was more than that. Los Angeles was more than his workplace. It was his home.

Later, Melvin left the party and flew back to his tree house. It had been a busy day. The McNasty Brothers were in prison once more, Melvin and his new assistant had escaped death, and now that it was over, he was tired–happy but tired. He knew he had to rest up for book number two.

Melvin munched pretzels and sipped root beer as he looked out over the lights of Los Angeles. Somewhere out there, trouble was brewing. He could feel it.

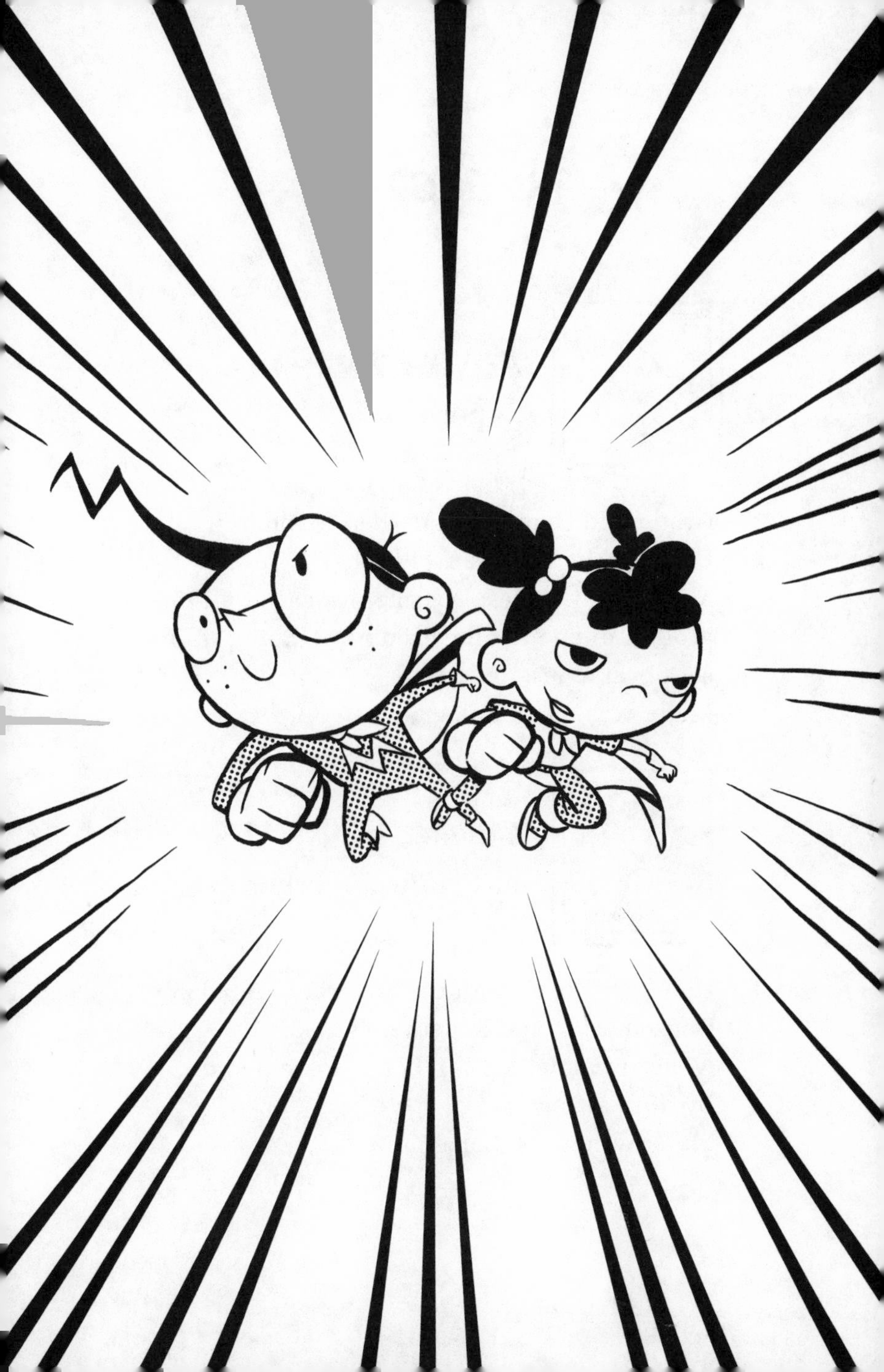

THE GOOD GUYS

MELVIN BEEDERMAN
Superhero

★ Graduated from the Superhero Academy
★ Lives by the Superhero's Code
★ Minor weaknesses: Doesn't always get off the ground in one try; has trouble stopping trains; sees everyone's underwear
★ Major weakness: Bologna

CANDACE BRINKWATER
Assistant Superhero

★ Didn't graduate from the Superhero Academy
★ Doesn't know the Superhero's Code
★ Minor weaknesses: Math; has to be home by dinnertime
★ Major weakness: Bologna

THE BAD GUYS

GRUNGE McNASTY

Notorious Bank Robber and
All-Around Bad Guy

* Leader of the McNasty Brothers
* What he loves: Loot (not money—loot)
* What he hates: Melvin Beederman
* Smells bad

FILTHY McNASTY

Notorious Bank Robber and
All-Around Bad Guy

* What he loves: Loot (not money—loot)
* What he hates: Melvin Beederman
* Smells worse than his brother

SUPERHERO'S CODE

1. Never say no to a cry for help
2. Find a good hideout
3. "Just doing my job, ma'am"
4. Know your weakness
5. Show up just in the nick of time
6. Always keep your cape clean
7. "Not so fast!"
8. Your brain is your greatest weapon
9. Believe in yourself at all times
10. Never break up a good team

130

WHO IS MELVIN BEEDERMAN?

Melvin Beederman wasn't always an orphan. No, indeed. He used to live with his math-genius father in a small apartment in Chicago. Day after day, Melvin watched his dad work complex word problems. In the evening, they would go out together in search of tasty snacks. Their favorite? Pretzels and root beer, of course.

One day, Mr. Beederman was working on the mother of all word problems. This thing was huge—and very difficult. It involved trains racing toward each other at different speeds. One of the trains was going so fast that it jumped the tracks and squashed him.

Poor Melvin became fatherless right then and there. He was placed in an orphanage, where he trudged and toiled until the day he was spotted by Headmaster Spinner. *A boy with noggin power*, thought the Headmaster. *The world could use a superhero like that!* And so young Melvin became Melvin Beederman, Superhero.

THE MAKING OF . . . MELVIN

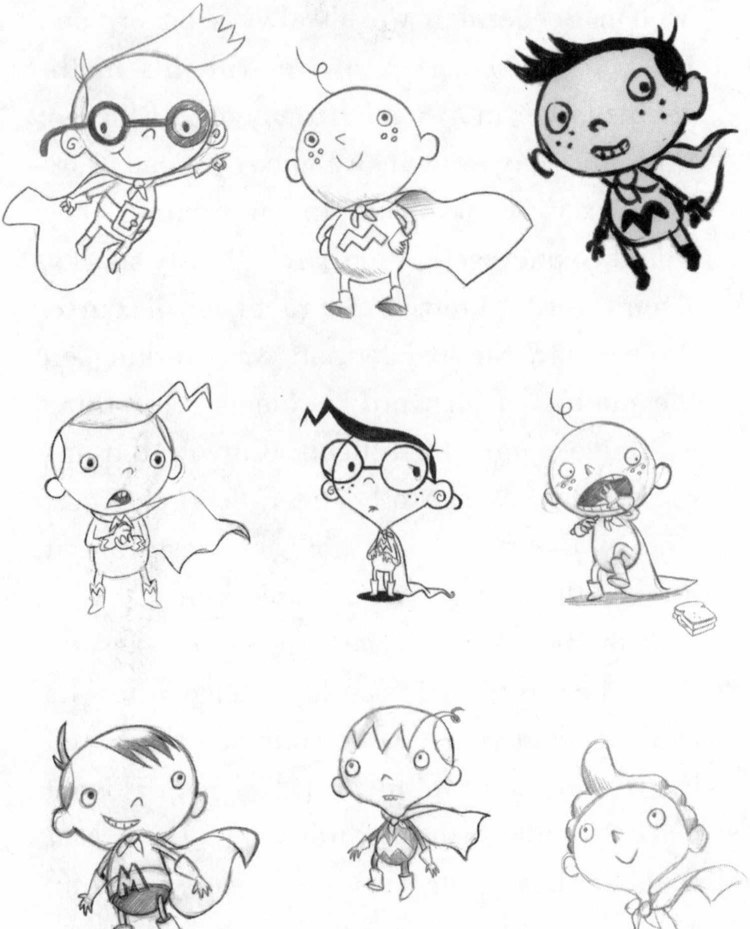

THE MAKING OF . . . CANDACE

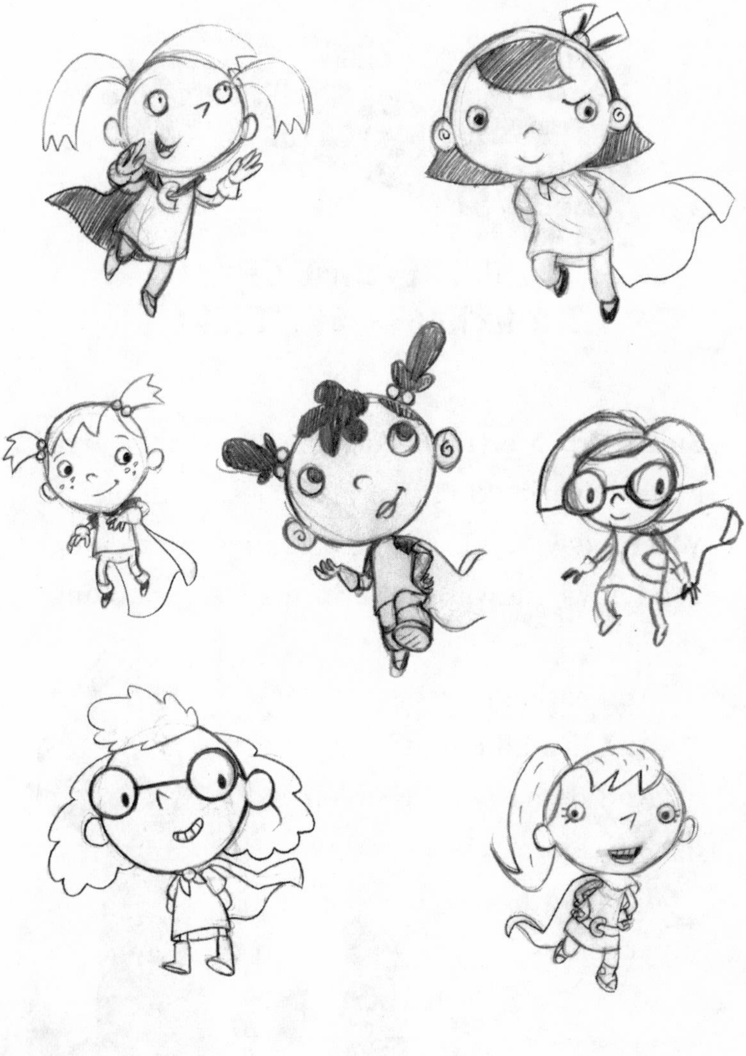

And now, a superheroic excerpt from

MELVIN BEEDERMAN SUPERHERO

THE REVENGE OF
THE McNASTY BROTHERS

Superhero Melvin Beederman lived in a tree house overlooking Los Angeles, California. When he wasn't catching bad guys or rescuing good guys, he was home in his tree, watching cartoons.

And eating pretzels.

And drinking root beer.

And doing math problems during commercials.

This is what superheroes

do when they're not working. The only thing that changes is the snack . . . and the math. Why was Melvin taking it so easy? Because the McNasty Brothers, those notorious bank robbers and all-around bad guys, were back in prison where they belonged. There were other bad guys who needed catching, of course. But they were not nearly as nasty as the McNasty Brothers.

They didn't smell as bad either.

So Melvin was taking a break, watching his favorite cartoon—*The Adventures of Thunderman.* Like most superheroes, Thunderman had an assistant. Her name was Thunder Thighs. Melvin Beederman also had an assistant: Candace Brinkwater. The only person ever to run the 100-yard dash in three and a half seconds. The only person ever to score 500 points in a basketball game. The only third-grader who could fly.

This flying stuff came in pretty handy for a superhero.

When *The Adventures of Thunderman* was over, Melvin typed an e-mail to his assistant.

Dear Candace,
Meet me at the library after school.
We'll do a little math, then catch some bad guys.
Sincerely,
Your partner in uncrime,
Melvin

This was their agreement: Melvin helped Candace with math, and she helped him save the world. Candace's parents loved having a daughter who saved the world on a regular basis—just as long as she was home for dinner.

Melvin pressed SEND on his computer. Suddenly, he heard something.

Squeak squeak.

Melvin jumped to his feet. He wasn't alone. "Who's there?"

Squeak squeak.

The squeaking was coming from behind the TV.

Melvin got ready to fight. "Whoever you are, come out with your hands up."

Wait a minute. That was policeman talk. And Melvin was a superhero, not a policeman. The squeaking intruder must have caught him off guard. He couldn't think.

"Come out and show yourself." *That's more like it,* Melvin thought. Superhero lingo. He'd learned the lingo along with the Superhero's Code at the academy. Years ago, he'd been plucked from an orphanage and sent there. And now he was on his own in Los Angeles, his first job since graduating. His tree house was his superhero's hideout—but maybe he wasn't as alone as he thought.

Squeak squeak.

He grabbed the TV and pushed it aside. Even though he stopped trains and outran bullets for a living, his heart was pounding.

Squeak squeak.

Melvin stared with his mouth open.

The intruder was nothing but a rat. A big rat, but a rat.

Melvin and the rat looked at each other. The rat wiggled his whiskers. Melvin didn't have any whiskers to wiggle. He wiggled his eyebrows instead.

"Hit the road, rat," Melvin said.

The rat didn't move.

"Take off. Scat. Beat it."

The rat stayed.

"Get out of—" Melvin stopped. Back at the Superhero Academy he could speak gerbil. And this rat was kind of like a gerbil. Four legs. A tail. Fur.

Melvin gave his eyebrows another wiggle. This was part of gerbil language. If he had whiskers he'd give them a shake. But eyebrows were all he had to work with. Then he said, "Squeak."